Echoes Don't Tell Lies

Neville Pettitt

ISBN:

By the Same Writer

1) **Turquoise & Other Shades of Blue** – October 2019
2) **Somewhere Behind These Eyes** – April 2020
3) **Victims of Indifference** – October 2020
4) **Beautiful Bruises** – November 2020
5) **The Logic of Fools** – May 2021
6) **Cotton Girls & Paper Chains** – January 2022
7) **Chasing Light** – January 2023
8) **Slaves of Eros a collection of love poems & erotica** – January 2023
9) **A Handful of Ghosts & A Woman in Blue** – October 2023

For my Beautiful Granddaughter

Astrid Wren Pettitt-Palmer

Table of Contents

Beyond All the Here's And All the Now's

Look beyond this very moment ..

Far beyond our

here's and nows and you shall

find a mighty

compilation of fables, foibles

and fantasies ..

As well as a few, magnificent

universal truths ..

Each far more than just a mere

token gesture ..

But which shall throw some light

upon the sheer

totality of my word blindness ..

Just Because She Is ..

If there were any more fitting words

than either beautiful, or perfect ..

Then I would not, for one single

moment, hesitate to use them here ..

Another Local Legend

Ever since he

began

repeating himself ..

His friends

began to call him

echo ..

Later, when he

began to talk to

himself

and in tongues ..

They all laughed

at him ..

Later still,

when he saw

something dark

in each

of them, they first

became

wary and then

very frightened

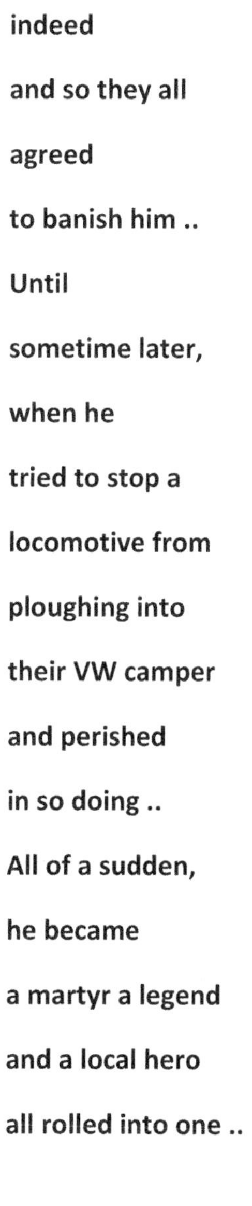

indeed

and so they all

agreed

to banish him ..

Until

sometime later,

when he

tried to stop a

locomotive from

ploughing into

their VW camper

and perished

in so doing ..

All of a sudden,

he became

a martyr a legend

and a local hero

all rolled into one ..

Neville Pettitt

I Think it Only Fair to Suggest

you are quite easily

my greatest regret ..

well at least you

would have been,

had you only ever

so much, as once

dared, to say yes ..

but I will be blowed

if I should ever

dare to ask you again ..

In a Muddle

Who knows

what is,

or what is not

allowed

these days ..

It seems to me

that maybe

no one knows ..

So perhaps,

that is why we

are all in

such an awful

fucking mess ..

No Contest

If you don't like losing

then don't let them beat you ..

It only ever becomes

a challenge darling ..

If you attempt to overcome,

to overthrow, or to defeat them ..

Shadows Don't Share Secrets

Shadows will never

share

your secrets darling ..

So surely

echo's won't tell

your lies ..

But the truth lies out

there

somewhere maybe ..

So pray

where did they go,

all those

people we once knew

and then,

with them, the cream

of our

years and our dreams ..

I do so fear

they might well have

all been,

somehow shadowed

away ..

Neville Pettitt

Outside Nikolai's Café Bar and Restaurant

I found her, or rather

she found me

outside Nikolai's café

bar and restaurant ..

It was, whatever it was,

depending on

the time of day or year

and what they had in ..

I was drinking

sun warmed beer,

she was sipping a long

ice cold green tea ..

It was near forty degrees

in the shade,

but there was no shade ..

She came over

and asked for a cigarette ..

I said I don't,

but thanks so very much

for asking ..

I'm not sure I know you

from Adam

though do I ma'am ..

She just smiled back at me

and so I gave her

what was left in the packet ..

Recall

Looking back then

now,

upon what might

well

once have been ..

Is not so

much a pleasant

lifestyle

choice these days ..

But rather

more, I am afraid

to say an

increasing necessity ..

When the Balance Wheel is Broken

when the balance wheel

is broken ..

when the main spring

has been sprung ..

when there are too many

complications

and when the date

and time are both wrong ..

maybe it's time

to think of saying goodbye

and though not

afraid of death or of dying

I need to die slower ..

since my fine house is not

yet In order ..

I need to post more first

class letters,

write that last poem down

and go wipe my

computer, before I say my

final goodbyes ..

Where Did She Go Before Breakfast

You simply could

not

like me any less

than

I dislike myself ..

Oh' you

are so very cruel

she said ..

He then looked in

her eyes

and smiled slow ..

No death

is free from pain,

he spat ..

But I assure you

thus, I would

not hurt a fly, nor

hair upon

your pretty head ..

Some say

she left him there

and then,

before she had her

breakfast ..

But one, at least

I'm sure,

knows very different ..

She May Have Been a Doppelganger After All

I swear I saw Meme Tereza

yesterday

waiting in a queue and praying

that the next flight

would depart on time

from gate fifteen, Tirana Airport ..

On second thoughts,

she may have just been asking

the day to be kind

to each and every single one of us ..

The plane though, was very much

delayed regardless ..

So I guess, she might have been

a doppelganger, after all ..

In the Wake of New Gods

Never fear my love

I could not

tear up, or otherwise

destroy all

the things that made

us look such fools ..

And anyway,

who am I to question

the validity

of your new god,

the latest iPhone

and your

unwavering devotion ..

Tomorrow

is another day

and in the meantime,

I shall take

a back seat for a while

and enjoy

what is left of the view

in the golden wake

of your brand new god ..

Neville Pettitt

Showing Off

Most perfectly attended

and likewise,

meticulously maintained ..

Her legs,

though barely parted yet,

her innocence

was deliberately displayed ..

Why They Called Him Bullet

once upon a time

that was,

I could easily cover

one hundred

yards, in less than

half the time

it now takes me

to bend

and tie a single shoe ..

Neville Pettitt

As Yet Unfurnished

Oh' so carelessly

discarded,

still warm to the touch

and likewise, strewn

with such magnificent

abandon ..

Across the well-trod

parquet polished floor

of our much used

yet otherwise,

still secret, rented room ..

When Absolutely Gone

When I am no more and gone ..

I want to be remembered

for the words I wrote, the deeds

I've done and for the love

I gave away and freely shared with

absolutely everyone ..

The Way it Was Not Long Ago

anyone over let's say

thirty five

and with a memory

that pre-dates

nineteen ninety seven

might well be

forgiven and better

understood ..

for their nightmares

and the flashbacks

they might

each experience ..

remembering hanged

men hanging

from street lamps

on the most

prominent of street

corners ..

and not a single beard

in sight ..

that is the way it was

back in the day ..

but then,

no one outside of that

dreadful regime

had the slightest clue

what was really going on ..

Who Needs Foreplay When We Got Poetry

From the very first
moment
they met ..
Part way
down and across
from
some hypothetical
empty page ..
Their love proved
unconventional ..
Yet it
remained
unconditional ..
Thus,
he said,
who needs words
these days
and what are they
worth anyway ..
Just some kind
of foreplay perhaps ..
When after all
said and done,

Echoes Don’t Tell Lies

what I desire

most,

is to make you go

uuh, aah aah ah ..

Oh’ yes,

yes, yes yes ..

In succinct terms

then ..

I so want us

to do this again

and again, sometime ..

Requiem For a Lost Cause

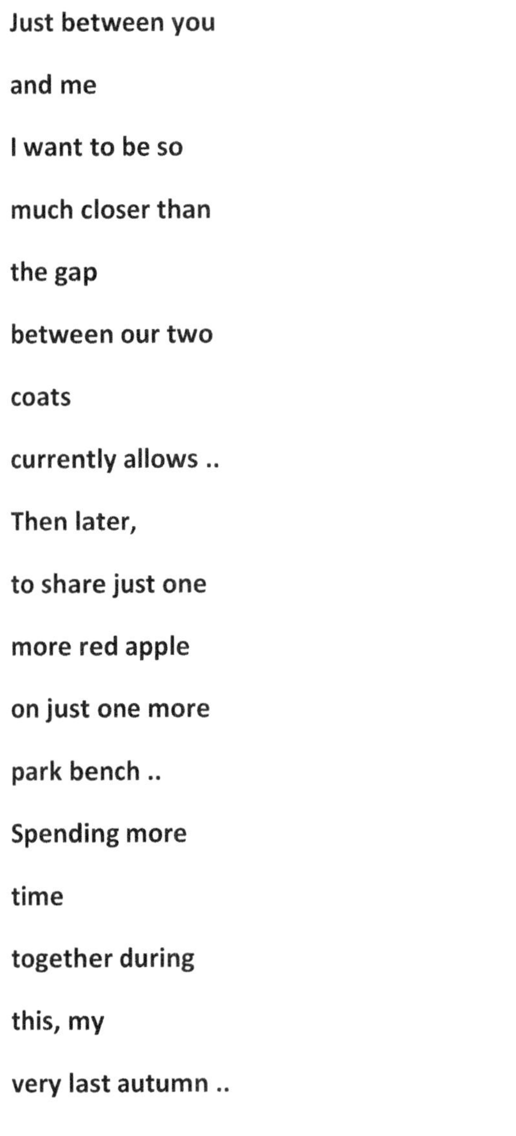

Just between you

and me

I want to be so

much closer than

the gap

between our two

coats

currently allows ..

Then later,

to share just one

more red apple

on just one more

park bench ..

Spending more

time

together during

this, my

very last autumn ..

These Words Have Nothing to Do With Weather

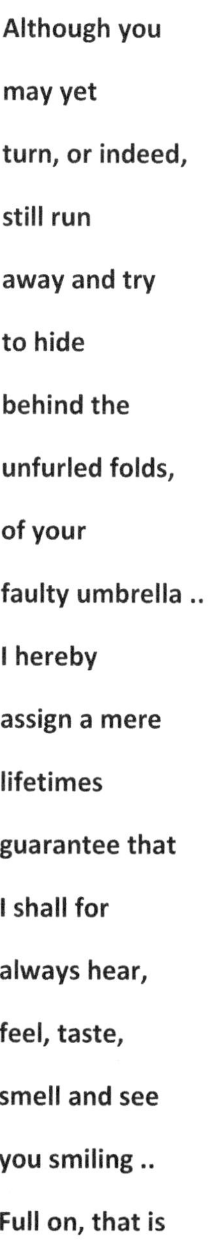

Although you

may yet

turn, or indeed,

still run

away and try

to hide

behind the

unfurled folds,

of your

faulty umbrella ..

I hereby

assign a mere

lifetimes

guarantee that

I shall for

always hear,

feel, taste,

smell and see

you smiling ..

Full on, that is

and through

the very many

tangled beards

and veils ..

Those, which

now line

the path on both

sides of this,

your most recent

of sainted

departures ..

And although

I should

not blame you

for the weather

darling ..

I know that in

all honesty ..

I most surely do

and for

so many other

things, besides ..

This Miserable Oubliette

Here, in this miserable oubliette

where they have consigned me ..

I shall wait patiently for you

to come hither and shit on me also ..

Some Things Are Best Left

There are some things

that should not be

seen, or heard or said

or done ..

I do not have to list

them here

now surely, do I, since

you will know

precisely what I mean ..

Such are the things

that each reside inside

our own

unique and individual

minds and thrive

in gutters everywhere ..

Smeared With Affection

Without any doubt

whatsoever ..

Your eyes, are my

spring my love

those that

somehow force me

to see beyond

the blues

and the greens ..

Yet while we are still

at the mercy

of such intimate liars

and fools ..

I swear I constantly

find myself

looking for colours ..

Indeed those,

that still live and do

thrive, someplace

else entirely ..

Pinned, albeit loosely

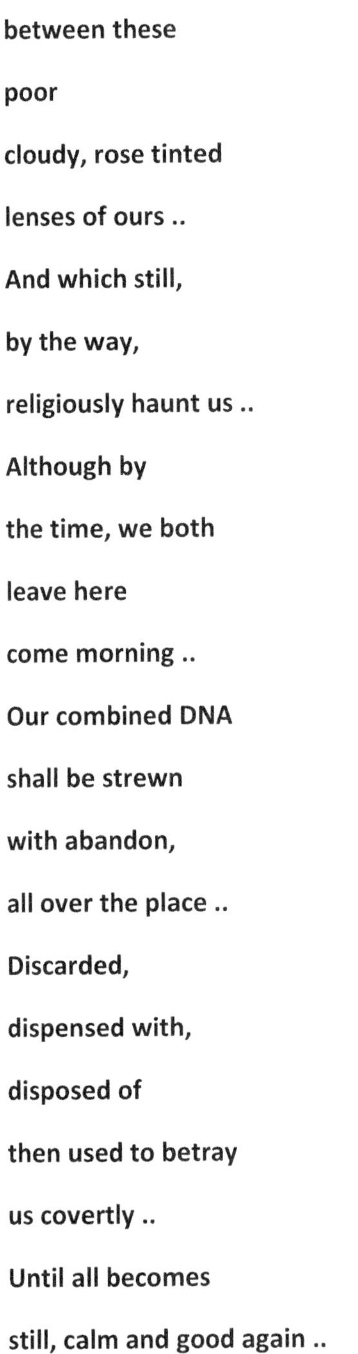

between these

poor

cloudy, rose tinted

lenses of ours ..

And which still,

by the way,

religiously haunt us ..

Although by

the time, we both

leave here

come morning ..

Our combined DNA

shall be strewn

with abandon,

all over the place ..

Discarded,

dispensed with,

disposed of

then used to betray

us covertly ..

Until all becomes

still, calm and good again ..

No More Fancy Restaurants

Now that you are gone

I dare say

nothing compared to you ..

Nothing

but trinkets, some vinyl

and a collection

of old, unfinished love songs ..

Tongue Spillage

Think hard upon

these words

that spill so freely

from this tongue ..

Like so very

many dandelion

clocks ..

Each blown from

here and there,

to kingdom come ..

And while I cannot

blame you

for the weather ..

I do blame you

for all those

silly lies you told ..

And likewise,

for many other

things besides ..

Like falling

in and out of love,

so very many times ..

Rank Order

Don't think for one moment

you might be second best ..

That would be ridiculous ..

Since you were, by no means

whatsoever, that high up the list ..

Barely Heard Through All The Whispers

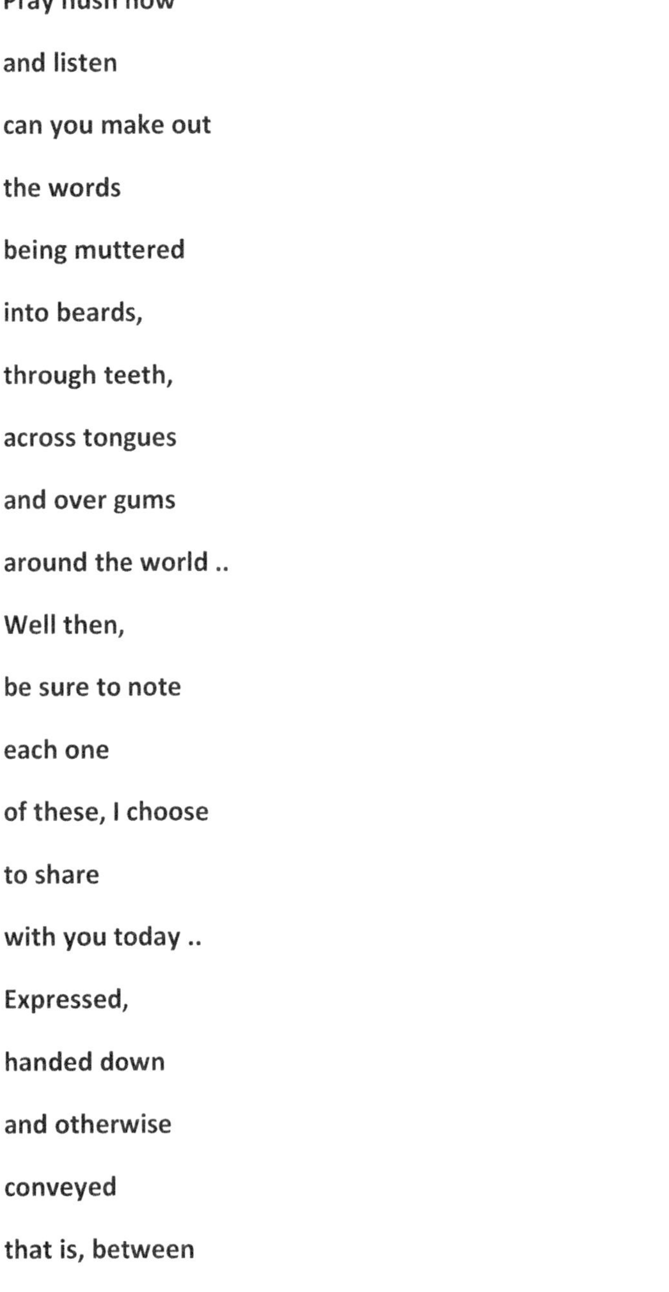

Pray hush now

and listen

can you make out

the words

being muttered

into beards,

through teeth,

across tongues

and over gums

around the world ..

Well then,

be sure to note

each one

of these, I choose

to share

with you today ..

Expressed,

handed down

and otherwise

conveyed

that is, between

one old

forbidden lover

and another ..

Now barely whispered ..

Why Else Wish Him So Blind

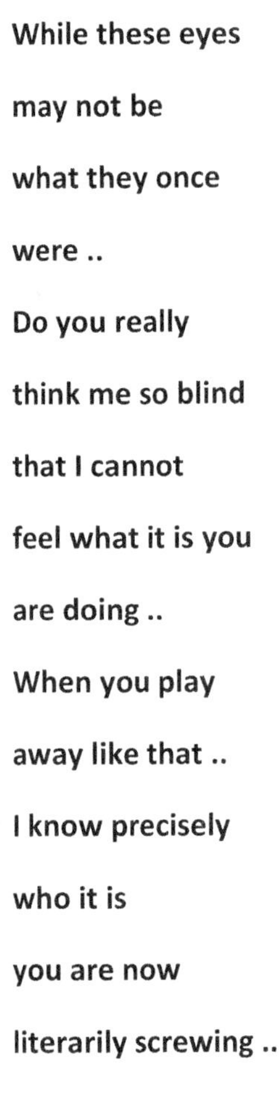

While these eyes

may not be

what they once

were ..

Do you really

think me so blind

that I cannot

feel what it is you

are doing ..

When you play

away like that ..

I know precisely

who it is

you are now

literarily screwing ..

Third Place

The gap between

silver and gold

was once, almost

indiscernible ..

Now though, after

all these years ..

There may always

be some doubt,

as to who took bronze ..

The Girl in a Red Bowler Hat

The girl in the red

bowler hat

made me smile

as she bounced

up and down

and waved from

the back

of her elephant ..

And then

again, as she

blew an innocent

kiss, in my

vague direction ..

But that was

so long ago now ..

When all the

colours held fast

and were in

the right places ..

Oh' such

halcyon days,

when I dreamt

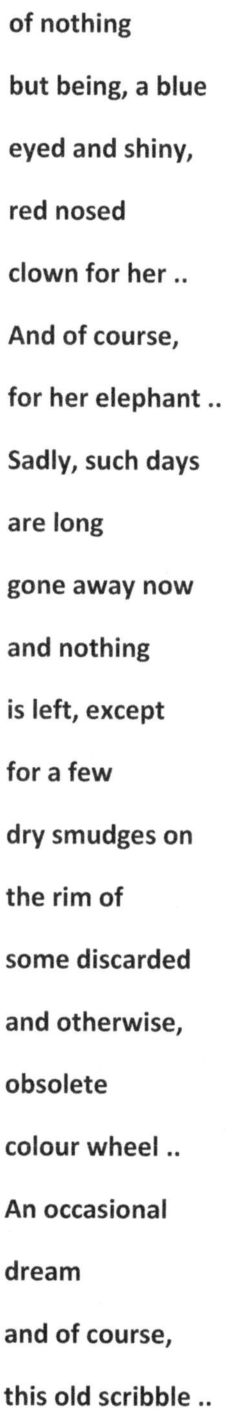

of nothing

but being, a blue

eyed and shiny,

red nosed

clown for her ..

And of course,

for her elephant ..

Sadly, such days

are long

gone away now

and nothing

is left, except

for a few

dry smudges on

the rim of

some discarded

and otherwise,

obsolete

colour wheel ..

An occasional

dream

and of course,

this old scribble ..

Impact

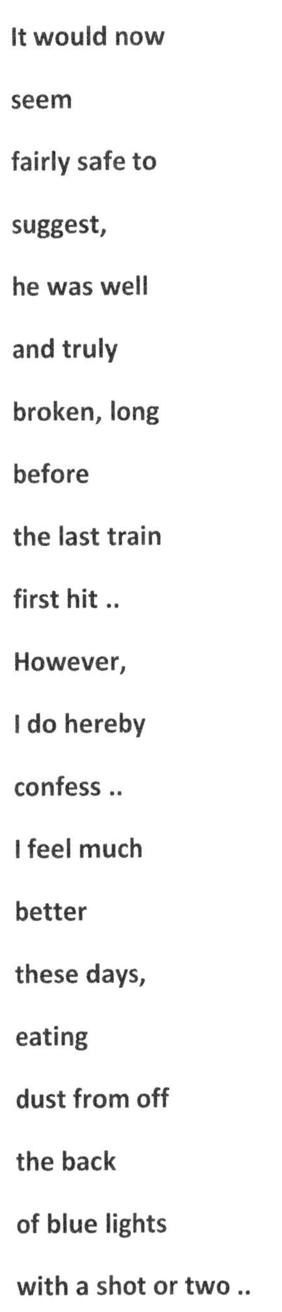

It would now

seem

fairly safe to

suggest,

he was well

and truly

broken, long

before

the last train

first hit ..

However,

I do hereby

confess ..

I feel much

better

these days,

eating

dust from off

the back

of blue lights

with a shot or two ..

Afterbirth

Gone in the blink

of a baby blue eye

that initial fear

filled micro moment

of awkwardness

new motherhood

invariably brings ..

Okay, so tears dried,

sighs sighed, milks

flowing and guess

what, babies cry ..

Isn't that the way

the text books say,

it should always be ..

Well listen folks

and hard, between

the sleep deprived

hallucinations

and let's not forget

the mood swings ..

Someone really needs

to say it, like it really is ..

Neville Pettitt

Don’t Kill The Coffee

Don’t you dare kill the coffee, she said ..

Pour the water on slow and then,

stir it clockwise, with love and affection ..

She was crazy like that, but I loved her

so much, and always called her mummy ..

Yesterday's Muse

She hides

and so well

behind

a makeshift

façade

of feigned

innocence,

hippy chick

tie dyed tops

and her

collection of

old torn

Victorian

lace ..

She lives in

some

kind of

smoke free,

and sterile

world of

gold gilded

fantasies,

yet she sucks

on Marlboro

lights

and tells lies ..

The kind

only a spoilt

child, or a

psychopath

might tell

on a bad hair

day ..

She cries a lot

too and at

the drop of

a hat ..

She still goes

to church on

Sundays tho' ..

Between

giving head,

that is

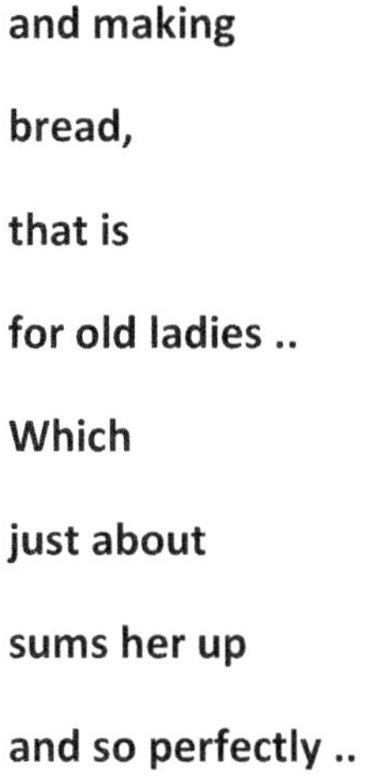

and making

bread,

that is

for old ladies ..

Which

just about

sums her up

and so perfectly ..

Steer Well Clear of Dorset Buoys

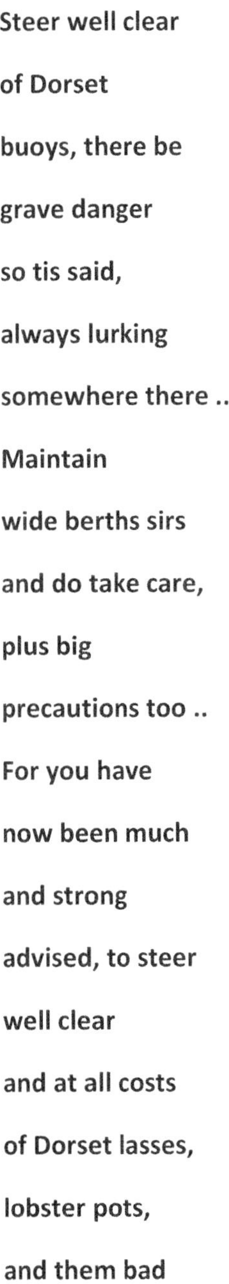

Steer well clear

of Dorset

buoys, there be

grave danger

so tis said,

always lurking

somewhere there ..

Maintain

wide berths sirs

and do take care,

plus big

precautions too ..

For you have

now been much

and strong

advised, to steer

well clear

and at all costs

of Dorset lasses,

lobster pots,

and them bad

Echoes Don't Tell Lies

old Dorset buoys ..

Indeed, the gulls

about yon

heads and flaxen

sails do cry ..

Be most afeared

of Bridport lads

and just as much

of West Bay too ..

If you do know

precisely, what is

good for all

brave young souls

and just as much,

be fearful for

your sorry crew ..

For she, the siren

has tis said,

one god almighty

appetite

and needs be fed,

she's far more

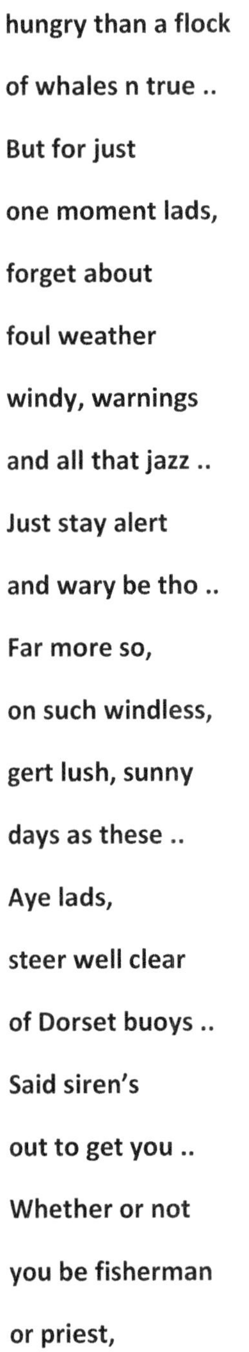

hungry than a flock

of whales n true ..

But for just

one moment lads,

forget about

foul weather

windy, warnings

and all that jazz ..

Just stay alert

and wary be tho ..

Far more so,

on such windless,

gert lush, sunny

days as these ..

Aye lads,

steer well clear

of Dorset buoys ..

Said siren's

out to get you ..

Whether or not

you be fisherman

or priest,

a boatbuilder,

soldier, baker or

some other

well-seasoned

salty sailor ..

Pray don't you

never forget this

well intentioned

saline, final warning ..

Odd Couples and Us

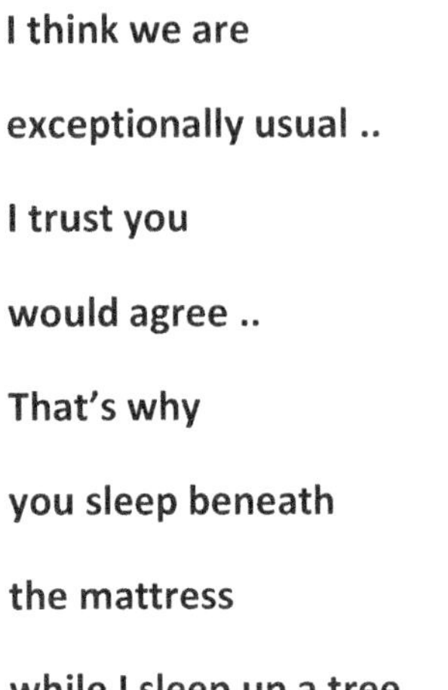

I think we are

exceptionally usual ..

I trust you

would agree ..

That's why

you sleep beneath

the mattress

while I sleep up a tree ..

Silverback

Dear lord,

tis just as feared ..

I look like

someone's grandpappy ..

Both with,

and without the beard,

that is ..

A silverback,

if ever there was ..

But by gum,

I am so very, very happy ..

The Day She Wore Flour in Her Hair

I saw her clearly edged

in golden light,

through sun rays poured

and filtered

through old stained glass ..

She had flour

in her hair and had been

baking bread ..

I simply cannot tell you,

just how hungry

we both then were, that day ..

Sibling Arrivalry

when she eventually

arrived ..

he so much wanted

to phone,

or rather, dash across

to his folks ..

with the glorious news

and to share,

his delight with them ..

but they were

both gone and he soon

remembered ..

he was still an orphan ..

oh' how he

envied oblivious siblings

that is .. until his

senses returned to him

later that day ..

and all was good again ..

Neville Pettitt

Two Unnecessary Evils

in a world of plenty

too many unnecessary evils

abide and thrive ..

of course, working and trading

on Sundays, are but two of them ..

Everyone a Loser

Take note,

she wins again

and everyone else loses ..

Well done, you made us losers too ..

But that's okay, by now, we are so used to it ..

For Astrid Wren, My Little Bird ..

Now you are here

we just can't

take our eyes of you ..

Yes you, and your

big baby blue eyes ..

Hey, just look at

those hands of hers

too tiny, to catch

hold of his fat thumb ..

She sounds

like a puppy, while

he stands there

on guard, beside her

just gazing down

and happily,

beating his drum ..

For she,

there is no doubt

at all, is loved,

perfect and beautiful

all neatly

rolled into one ..

It was then, that he

cried through his

whiskers

and he whispered ..

I shall be brave for you

Astrid,

my dear Astrid Wren ..

Just for you,

my little bird, I shall

forever be wise

and always, be strong ..

Indeed,

all the time

not just now and then ..

Neville Pettitt

A Thought For a Day

every single day is special

for someone, somewhere, surely ..

Somewhere off The M35

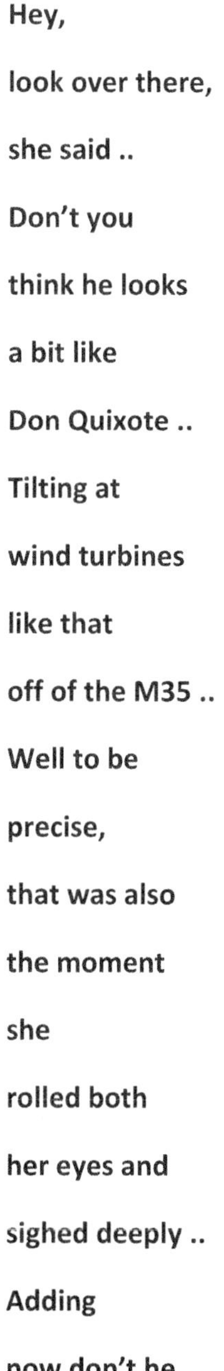

Hey,

look over there,

she said ..

Don't you

think he looks

a bit like

Don Quixote ..

Tilting at

wind turbines

like that

off of the M35 ..

Well to be

precise,

that was also

the moment

she

rolled both

her eyes and

sighed deeply ..

Adding

now don't he

look totally

fit and divine ..

No, not

on your nelly,

he looks

a right proper

twat ..

Her best mate

in the whole

widest

world, swiftly

replied ..

And I would

so much

prefer it if he

be yours,

rather than mine ..

Sweet Salted Caramel Eyes

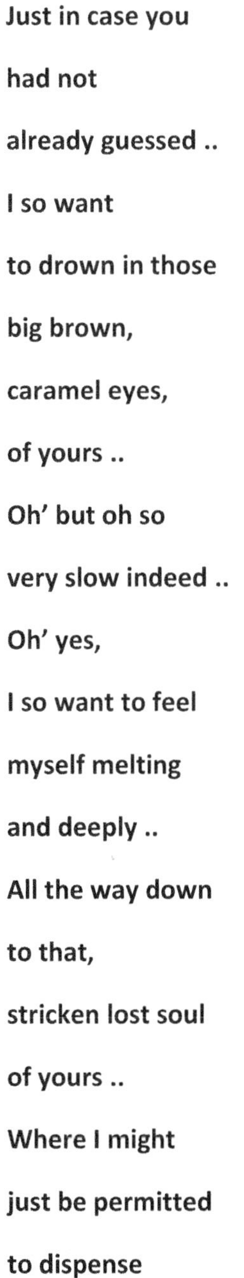

Just in case you

had not

already guessed ..

I so want

to drown in those

big brown,

caramel eyes,

of yours ..

Oh' but oh so

very slow indeed ..

Oh' yes,

I so want to feel

myself melting

and deeply ..

All the way down

to that,

stricken lost soul

of yours ..

Where I might

just be permitted

to dispense

once and for all

with this searching ..

To discard

the weight of my

longing

and to finally feel,

for once at least,

that innermost

heat of you darling ..

A Moment of Enlightenment

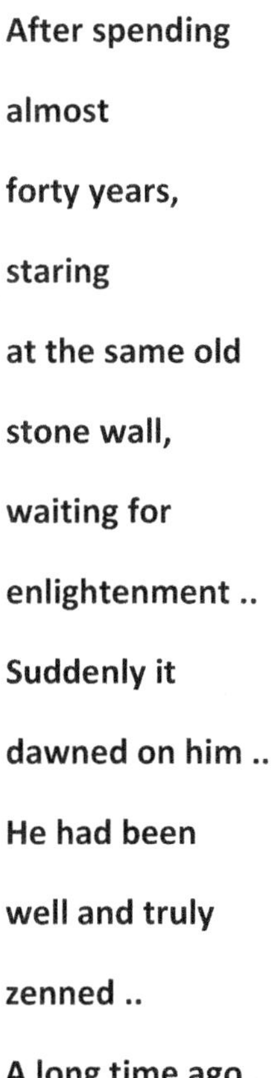

After spending

almost

forty years,

staring

at the same old

stone wall,

waiting for

enlightenment ..

Suddenly it

dawned on him ..

He had been

well and truly

zenned ..

A long time ago ..

Mused

It was that last
verse
that killed him ..
As indeed,
all last verses
seemed to do ..
But then,
once he had
died,
just a little bit ..
He took
one final deep
breath,
filled his pen
and lay down ..
It was
high time he
thought,
that his muse
should
take over again ..

Briefly Interrupted by Sleep

This is not a turning point,

a parking place or reversing bay ..

It is nothing, but a brief red light stop

at the end, of yet another, very busy day ..

Neville Pettitt

Brûlée

Round and round and round

she goes

with her wagging tail and ever

twitching nose ..

Yet rarely

does she put her bottom down ..

But that's

the way it always bloomin goes

Oh' yes indeed,

that's none other than, our Brûlée

for you ..

Sitting at the foot of our stairs,

panting heavy

and with that cold and ever

twitching nose ..

Always ready to explode,

should a ball,

a postman, or a squirrel ever dare

to show ..

That's Brûlée, Bru, Bruiser, Parsley,

Parsnip Pettitt for ya ..

Squeezed Between Our Now and Thens

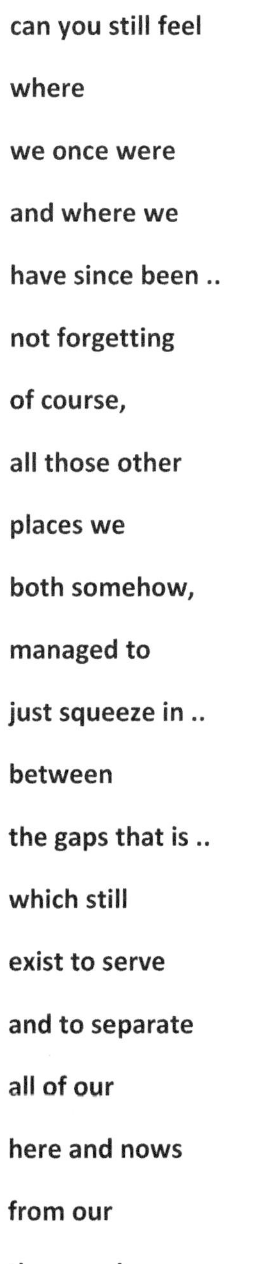

can you still feel

where

we once were

and where we

have since been ..

not forgetting

of course,

all those other

places we

both somehow,

managed to

just squeeze in ..

between

the gaps that is ..

which still

exist to serve

and to separate

all of our

here and nows

from our

there and our

thens ..

I know I still do,

albeit occasionally ..

Fear Silence Not

Do not fear silence

my friend,

there is nothing

to be afraid of there ..

For it is long

empty like discarded

worm casts

and old redundant

conch shells ..

Filled only with echo's

and the laughter

of long ago moments ..

Still occasionally

carried before the tides

and the winds

of yesterday's gone ..

And as such,

there is nothing to fear

whatsoever ..

Neville Pettitt

Whispered

no one was looking

so he hid

a whispered secret

deep

within the perfect

folds

of the new babies

ear ..

and she smiled back

at him ..

knowing for sure

in that

whisp of a whisper ..

she was

more than just merely

loved ..

A Slice of Sky

Pastel

amethyst yellow

skies ..

Filled to overflow

with the

silhouettes

of gold eyed birds

in flight ..

I must make notes ..

For surely,

winter is only just

around,

the very next corner ..

Neville Pettitt

Recollecting Unusual Positions

Simultaneously

looking down at her back

through the hull

of a glass bottomed boat

and up at the soles

of her feet and her skirts

from where he lay

in the gutter of some god

forsaken city or other ..

Anyone watching

would have thought it was

magic, or witchcraft

or something entirely not

of this earth ..

And they would have been

right of course,

since he was in the process

of dying alone

in that gutter, with just a few

fading photographs

and a memory or two of her ..

Let's Play Sushi

She lounged like

a reptile

lounges, draped

and long

beside the hastily

discarded

kimono and pink

flip flops ..

Soaking up those

excess rays

and smiling behind

the shades ..

Today she is a slick

green

chameleon with an

opal pinned

to each of her shell

like ears ..

Sipping slow on chilled

rice wine

and playing chase

Neville Pettitt

around

the rim of a china

dinner plate

with her lovers sushi ..

All Bases Covered

her name formed

but a small

part of the litany

he once

wrote for her ..

and which,

he would mouth

over and over ..

indeed,

she was recited

and sung

and then pinned

with such

pride to the walls

of great temples,

majestic

cathedrals and a

few scattered

shrines

here and there

for PR

purposes and just

to ensure

all known tick boxes

had each

been suitably crossed ..

Would You Kindly Pass the Entonox Babe

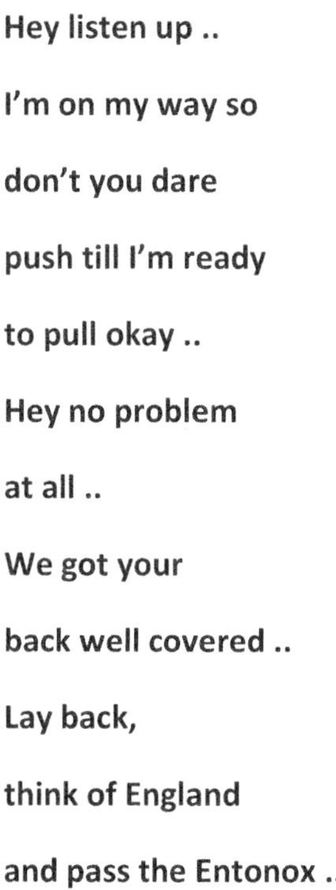

Hey listen up ..

I’m on my way so

don’t you dare

push till I’m ready

to pull okay ..

Hey no problem

at all ..

We got your

back well covered ..

Lay back,

think of England

and pass the Entonox ..

Neville Pettitt

While Out Busy Partying

He was not good enough

for her, but she

was far too good for him ..

Yet my how her

bones they did rattle like

a sack filled

with old rusty spanners

or something ..

She had not got one single

ounce of meat,

on her at all, but he liked

her like that

and she swore she would

never dare to

get fat and risk losing him ..

Sadly, she passed

recently as he, so they say ..

Was out on

the town busy boozing and

partying and

fucking her cousin, the whole night, clean away ..

For little j always remembered with BIG love and much respect ..

Shallow Cuts Too Deep

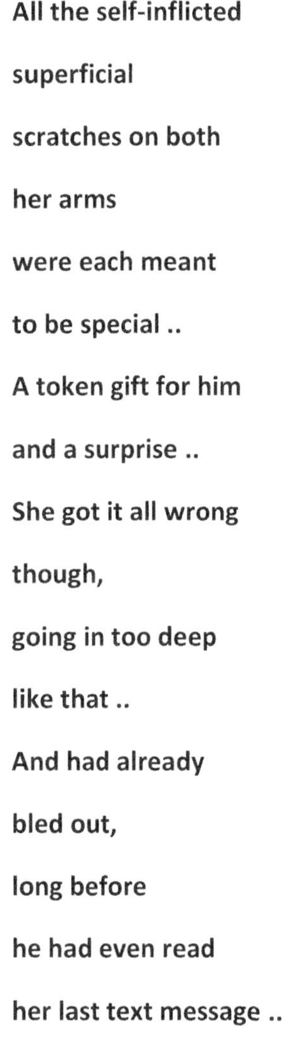

All the self-inflicted

superficial

scratches on both

her arms

were each meant

to be special ..

A token gift for him

and a surprise ..

She got it all wrong

though,

going in too deep

like that ..

And had already

bled out,

long before

he had even read

her last text message ..

Scammed

What kind of scam

are you running ..

I hope it's about us

making love

and not just about

making money ..

There's far too much

hypocrisy,

selfishness and lies

going on all

around us, these days ..

Imagine

Can you imagine

a world

without justice,

compassion,

poetry or love ..

Hell no,

she sighed ..

Well neither

can we

so that's it then ..

We shall

say our goodbyes

and then get

right out of here ..

Id

she needs to be wanted
almost as much as
she wants to be needed ..

in fact, sadly even more
so perhaps ..
it is such a crying shame ..

she never seems to learn
from all her silly
and avoidable mistakes ..

and should you ever think
I care at all now
then you really are deluded ..

Neville Pettitt

Critical Observations

Every now and then

while reading between the lines,

words become superfluous

Colour Envy

The following words

are for those

for whom, colours

no longer matter ..

For those

who may yet still

be indelibly

bruised, or stained

by desire

and by their very

own passion ..

Each of the words

which now

follow and truly

are for those,

blown away by

beauty

and an urgent,

uncertain longing ..

Indeed all

of the following

words are meant

solely for

those, who might

be intent

upon breaking

each fresh new

disciple ..

Before removing

of course,

all traces of old

colour and now,

obsolete predecessors ..

Crying Shame

She so much
needs to be
wanted in fact
twice as much
if not more
than she wants
to be needed ..
And likewise
be adored ..
It is therefore
such a crying
shame that she
never seems to
get bored or to
learn from all of
her silly mistakes ..

Neville Pettitt

Bang Goes Another Theory

There is something electromagtastic

about the old dust

collecting on new computer screens ..

There is something

about the destruction found in re-birth

and the proceeds of

artificially impregnated intelligence seeds ..

There is something

in all of the aps and the ampules that we

now find discarded

and littering our almost everywheres ..

I so hope you can feel

the enormity and asceticism of what I mean ..

Once Upon Her Night Scented Garden

some time

during the night,

I quit kicking

dead leaves

and threw away

my secateurs ..

that was

not long before

I stumbled

upon those old

red brick steps ..

all eight of them

if my memory

serves correctly ..

and those,

which then led

to your most

secret of gardens ..

long before

that is, the pink

those gold

and the cream

anemones ..

together with

the topiary bay

and a sweet

night scented

jasmine

all got together

and held me

as their hostage ..

Best Not Let it Fester

I always tend

to find,

if I say it, like it

really is ..

I generally feel,

one hell

of a lot better

right afterwards ..

The Measure of a Single Year

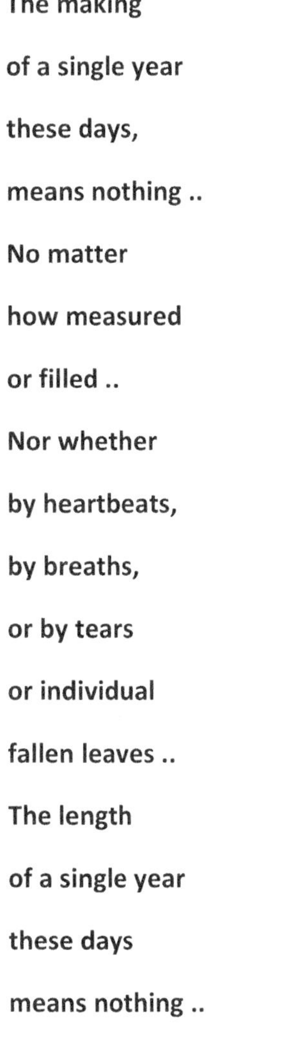

The making

of a single year

these days,

means nothing ..

No matter

how measured

or filled ..

Nor whether

by heartbeats,

by breaths,

or by tears

or individual

fallen leaves ..

The length

of a single year

these days

means nothing ..

Along Non Parallel Lines

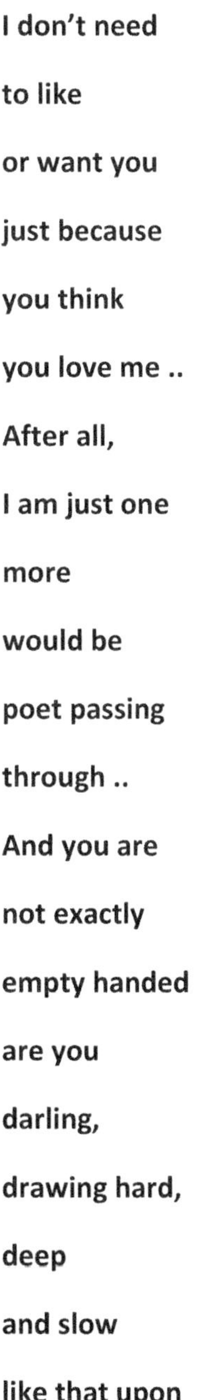

I don't need

to like

or want you

just because

you think

you love me ..

After all,

I am just one

more

would be

poet passing

through ..

And you are

not exactly

empty handed

are you

darling,

drawing hard,

deep

and slow

like that upon

your cork

tipped French

cigarette ..

Are we not

just running

on empty

along these

pseudo

non parallel

lines ..

Where it just

occurred

to me, I don't

need to like or to

love you after all ..

The Making of a Single Murmuration

At precisely

the same time

three

thousand

tiny heartbeats

began to

flutter here

and there ..

Six thousand

sky hungry

wings began

to dance as one ..

Across

the compelling

turquoise skies

and in all

directions too ..

Each smiling high

above and then

down upon our

very own

secret orchard ..

Surely seen

by other mortal

eyes somewhere ..

And likewise,

murmurized

oh' yes indeed,

as were, my very own ..

Shrewsbury Folk

There is something

pretty awesome,

and not just pretty

about two

thousand individual

upturned

umbrella's like that ..

Each pinned

upside down, to the

roof of a marque

the same colour as

festival sky ..

No, my dear friend,

it was

most definitely not,

just one

more rainbow in the

making ..

But one made with

so much

love by all of them

goodly

old Shrewsbury folk ..

For the likes

of all those, you n me ..

Well Blocked Babe

Its three thirty four in

the morning

and the beginning of

yet another

miserable September ..

I'm just writing

a few notes up before

checking

in on the weather

and although it is warm

here, I am

laughing my socks off ..

Because all

your so called friends

are now saying,

you've only recently

blocked me ..

Oh' how I do hope so,

because

I blocked you, long ago ..

But of course,

I shall never find out

for sure ..

Because I won't even

bother to check anyway ..

And that goes

to show, just how little

you do mean to me now ..

My Country is Falling Apart At the Seams

my country is
falling apart
at the seams,
she is broken
and failing
in so many
places,
you would
hardly believe.
but I dare not
let go of her yet
still I doubt
it will be
that long
before we are
nothing more
than a smudge
on an old map
somewhere
perhaps
my country

is a train crash

just waiting to

happen, she has

been beaten

defeated and

long since cowed ..

What a Covert Waste of Space

looking down on me and you
she lives in a world, way too fast
while forever, running on empty ..

that is precisely, where she hides,
behind ciphers and codes, but grapes
and diet coke, won't keep her thin tho ..

Neville Pettitt

Just a Little Bit Famous

She so needs to be noticed,

she so wants to be watched ..

She is just a little bit famous,

but not too keen, to be touched ..

Sans Everything

Don't cry for her now, she has lost almost everything,

although tis true, she never wanted, most of it anyway ..

It still seems, she brought much of it, upon herself ..

Poor thing, it's all going so very wrong for her these days,

sans love, sans beauty, sans uterus, sans everything ..

Dick and the Swearmonger's Daughter

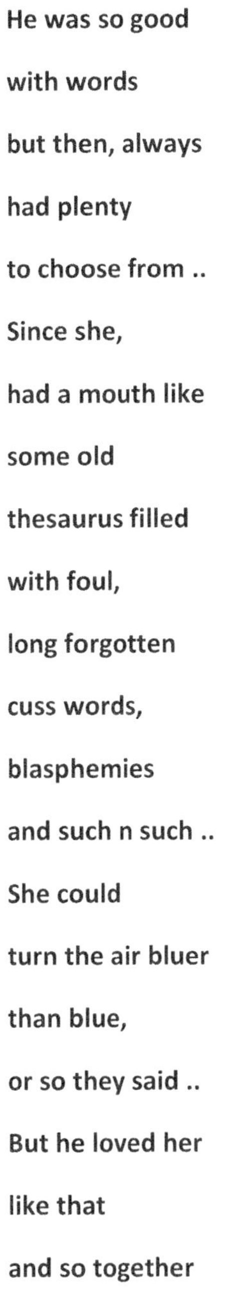

He was so good

with words

but then, always

had plenty

to choose from ..

Since she,

had a mouth like

some old

thesaurus filled

with foul,

long forgotten

cuss words,

blasphemies

and such n such ..

She could

turn the air bluer

than blue,

or so they said ..

But he loved her

like that

and so together

they sat ..

Making up new

rude words,

for nowt but

their own sense

of fun and of

course, the very

coarse crack of it ..

On Returning to Gullworthy

There is an old stone bridge,

somewhere

way over yonder, that still

crosses our Tamar ..

Some way before she reaches

weirhead and where

the salmon, still leap in threes ..

There is also a hovel,

well hidden behind brambles

and bracken,

where old Betsy Drury once

lived and cast spells ..

I note there is too, a derelict

cowshed still

barely standing and where

more than once,

we played doctors and nurses,

in old Dodges field ..

Oh' my word folks, it feels I've

been away for years ..

Yet in spite of all that, I think

I might just have

caught sight of her recently ..

Still wearing a smile,

an Afghan, her beads and her flares ..

Neville Pettitt

Whatever Happened to Miriam

There are still times I wonder,

whatever

happened to Miriam

our most

beautiful, of water carriers ..

She had

her own secrets, of course ..

But hey,

didn't we all, back then ..

Yet I seem

to recall a long time ago now

I once had

her naked, while standing

alone by

a fountain with her broken

decanter ..

Only half-filled mind, with

herbs and wild

honey like some enchanted

cornucopia

and likewise, so very inviting ..

Echoes Don't Tell Lies

My word,

how she smiled at me then,

whilst slowly

replacing, the cream coloured

hand woven

shawl, back over her shoulders

and blowing

a kiss in my vaguest direction ..

All before

turning and so very casually,

walking away ..

The Rape of the Wreck Known As M257

The stricken craft

M257 lay stuck

hard and fast upon

her leeward side ..

With fore mast split

from top

through to her tail

waiting on the tide ..

No colours

would she fly again

nor proudly

sail our seven seas ..

She's waiting

on the salvage crew

to strip her clean

of cargo, ballast

and any bounty hid

they may

yet chance to find

stowed inside

a beach holed hull

and all along her

splintered oaken seams ..

Bell Bottom Blues

Somewhere

up

Manchester

way

apparently,

they

still say that

there's

just enough

blue,

left in the sky ..

To make

a sailor, a new

pair of

old trousers ..

She Wore Him So Well

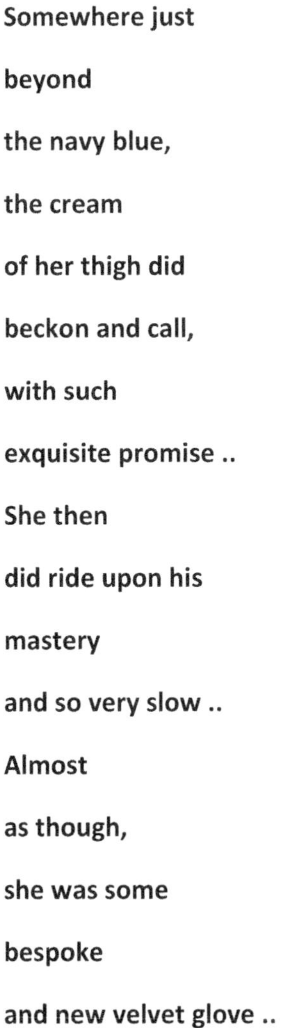

Somewhere just

beyond

the navy blue,

the cream

of her thigh did

beckon and call,

with such

exquisite promise ..

She then

did ride upon his

mastery

and so very slow ..

Almost

as though,

she was some

bespoke

and new velvet glove ..

So Long Marion

He waved so long to

his Marion ..

As Jane happened

to be travelling through ..

She claimed,

it was just coincidence ..

Since she was

passing alone and along

on that very

same route, anyway too ..

Why Not Just Call it a Day

At the end of a very long day

and if you still think, you are calling the shots

let's do each other a favour and just call it a day, full stop ..

Neville Pettitt

Glow

she had a strange light

all about her,

which she wore like a

pair of drawn

curtains, to let all her

shadows

breathe easy, she said ..

and while

those she did cast both

fore and aft,

appeared golden, not

one of her

disciples then glowed ..

but in that

moment she stumbled

and fell, each

one of those disciples

could tell she

was far from perfect

and her robe

was but sackcloth, hastily

throwed ..

Dearth

Can you feel

the weight of my

longing ..

It is greater than

when I lost blue ..

And so

I now wonder,

where on earth,

did the sky

all go, when you

left me

alone with my

hunger ..

Tho' should we

by chance,

ever meet again

my love ..

I am sure I would

more than

just disappoint ..

Yes again

and again, until

all the cows

have come home

and you had

lost what was

left of your appetite ..

Not Guilty as Charged

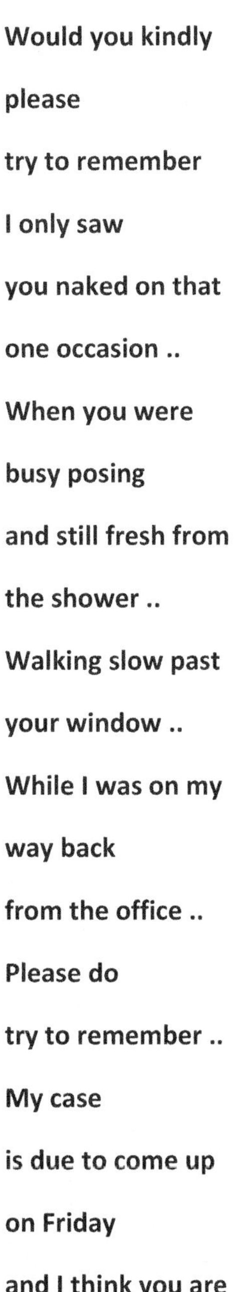

Would you kindly

please

try to remember

I only saw

you naked on that

one occasion ..

When you were

busy posing

and still fresh from

the shower ..

Walking slow past

your window ..

While I was on my

way back

from the office ..

Please do

try to remember ..

My case

is due to come up

on Friday

and I think you are

ugly anyway ..

So why

would you even

begin to think that

I might be stalking you ..

Just a Few Odd Diary Notes

Each of the following brief notes

was covertly removed from the

long diary of a very short lived man ..

Seafood and eat it

See her and run like hell

Seasons we must be getting older ..

Now surely two out of three aint bad ..

But then, at the end of the day

who's counting anyway ..

Decline

I have noticed in

the last month or so

marked changes ..

You are no longer

pretty even ..

In fact, far from it ..

I sometimes

wonder if you ever

really were ..

I used to love those

long pleated

skirts you wore

though ..

But now, I'm afraid

you would

be hard pushed

to even make,

an ill-fitting body

stocking look special ..

Once Upon a Fairy Tale True

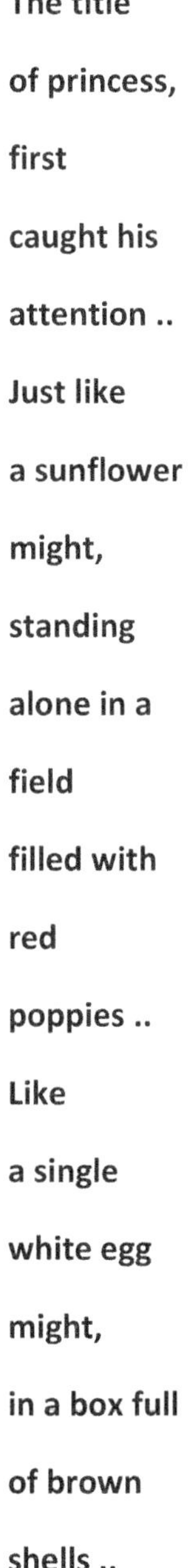

The title

of princess,

first

caught his

attention ..

Just like

a sunflower

might,

standing

alone in a

field

filled with

red

poppies ..

Like

a single

white egg

might,

in a box full

of brown

shells ..

And in that

briefest

of moments

he did fall

madly

in love with

her as she

did with he ..

So got

married the

very next

day and then

had three

sons and a

daughter ..

And went on

to live

very happily,

for ever after ..

Non Figmental

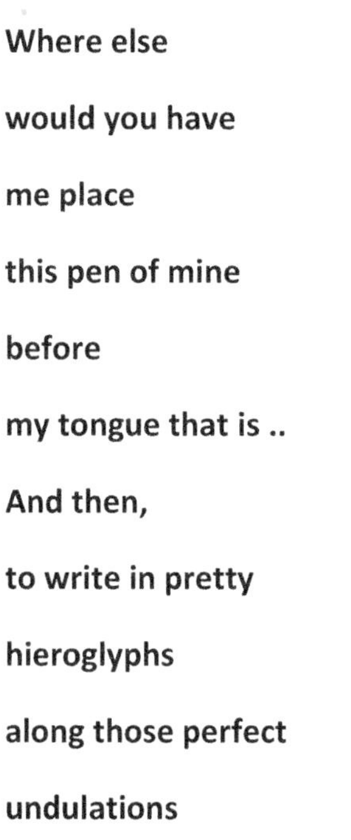

Where else

would you have

me place

this pen of mine

before

my tongue that is ..

And then,

to write in pretty

hieroglyphs

along those perfect

undulations

of your exquisite spine ..

Neville Pettitt

A Few Things Missed But in No Particular Order

He was good

with wood ..

He was good

with just about

everything ..

Except maybe

electricity ..

Which he kept

clear of ..

But boy was he

damn good

with any kind

of wood ..

After all, when

he lived by

the sea he was

a master

boatbuilder ..

But later,

when forced

to come ashore

Echoes Don't Tell Lies

he became

just one more

old carpenter ..

And once

in every while

an inventor too ..

Just for the

bloody hell of it ..

In fact,

I seem to recall

we played

checkers with

the trellis

he took off a

wall in our old

garden

and lay flat on

the flags

in Grandma's

courtyard ..

Hey, what could

have possibly

been any

better than that

with a bottle

of pop and a

packet of crisps

plus a tiny

blue parcel of salt ..

The Joining of Frayed and Loose Ends

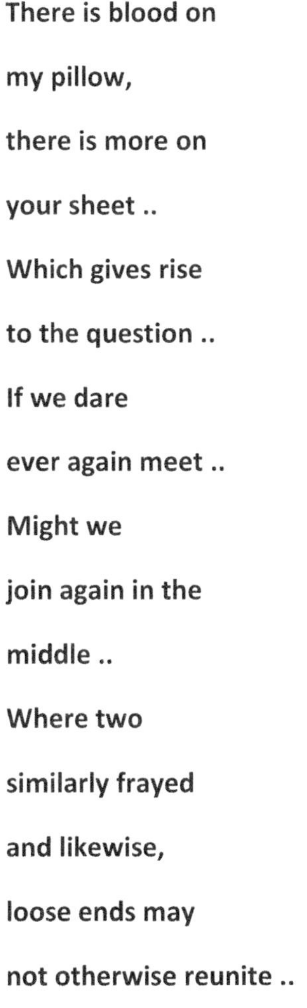

There is blood on

my pillow,

there is more on

your sheet ..

Which gives rise

to the question ..

If we dare

ever again meet ..

Might we

join again in the

middle ..

Where two

similarly frayed

and likewise,

loose ends may

not otherwise reunite ..

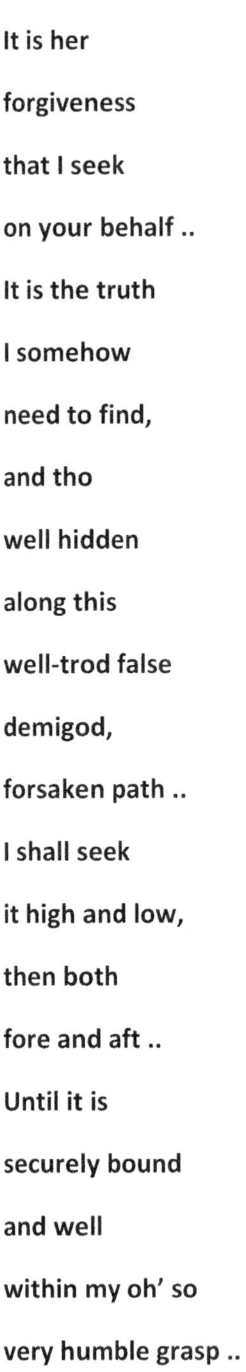

As Yet to Be

It is her

forgiveness

that I seek

on your behalf ..

It is the truth

I somehow

need to find,

and tho

well hidden

along this

well-trod false

demigod,

forsaken path ..

I shall seek

it high and low,

then both

fore and aft ..

Until it is

securely bound

and well

within my oh' so

very humble grasp ..

With No Cage to Hold Her She Learnt How to Fly

He spent half

his life

making out

she was

the one in the

wrong ..

But the longer

the silence,

the sadder her

song became ..

And tho'

he regrets it

all now ..

All the more

chronic

the ache

became also ..

So he chose

to unlock

the cage and

leave the

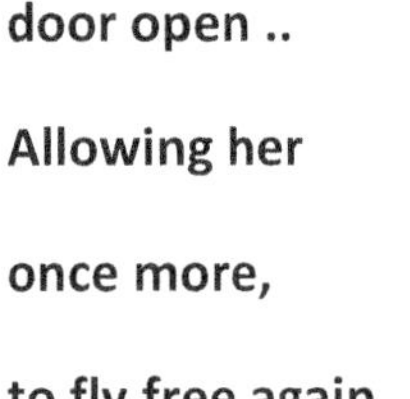

door open ..

Allowing her

once more,

to fly free again ..

Me and My Long List of Things

Hey, I once had a thing about each of the following ..

wristwatches

cheese

birds

sun dried tomatoes

anchovies

sun warmed sake

clocks

honesty

leather soled shoes

being on time

red wine

bizarre destinations

seafood

mirrors

doors

windows

justice

Oh' and of course poetry ..

So I wrote you this list, to remember, or to imagine me by ..

As a Matter of Fact It's a Fact

If I should

dare

to live just

long

enough to

pay

off all the

interest ..

Then

I shall die

a very

happy man

indeed

and not

in any debt ..

It's Not What it Used to Be

Well that's that

then,

one more

summer gone ..

Thirteen

whole days

of partial sun ..

Not in a row

though,

but scattered

so very

randomly

between May

and September ..

Not like

it used to be

when we

were so young ..

Neville Pettitt

Something About Shells

There is something

about shells,

the nature and form

of them ..

The way that they

capture

the ocean and sound

of her voice ..

There is something

about shells,

the weight and feel

of them

as they do call to us,

o'er the cry

of desperate gulls ..

Yes indeed,

there is something

a tiny bit

special about shells,

as they lay

empty and waiting to

haunt us

with the call, the kiss

and the

mighty roar of the sea

..

Miss. Esme G. Cameron

Despite the fact she
knew all
the Latin names for
garden plants
and was a dab hand
at ikebana ..
She also played viola,
flute and piano ..
Every now and then,
she would also
appear in church on
Sundays
and was renowned
for writing a
occasional novel ..
It is said
she may have looked
like a nun
and dressed like some
old librarian
but she thought and

Echoes Don't Tell Lies

wrote like a

well-versed dockyard

hooker ..

Although to be fair,

somewhere

beneath her pince-nez,

the tartan shawl

and tweeds, our not yet

quite famous

Miss. Grace Pratt didn't

only sweat,

but she also, did bleed

some of the

most exquisite poetry

you are ever

likely to read and the

more risqué,

the better it seemed ..

But then that was her

secret you see ..

At times in-between

her verses

and stanza's or prose,

only a handful,

the privileged few, ever

knew she

would occasionally puff

on a cigar,

or one of those French

cigarettes,

that she always kept in

a drawer filled

with old fountain pens,

a few saucy postcards

and a single

letter marked Flanders,

France 1918 ..

Grace Pratt helped me

one hell of a lot

while I was growing up

and falling in

love with this beautiful

beast that we

each all, call poetry ..

But the reason

I write now, is I recently

read that

Miss. Esme G. Cameron

formally known

as Grace Pratt, died at

home in

her sleep then aged one

hundred

and one whole year's

young, but who's counting ..

Because she was worth it

And for anyone who might be interested, Esme G. Cameron was Grace's pen name

Peck Drop and Run

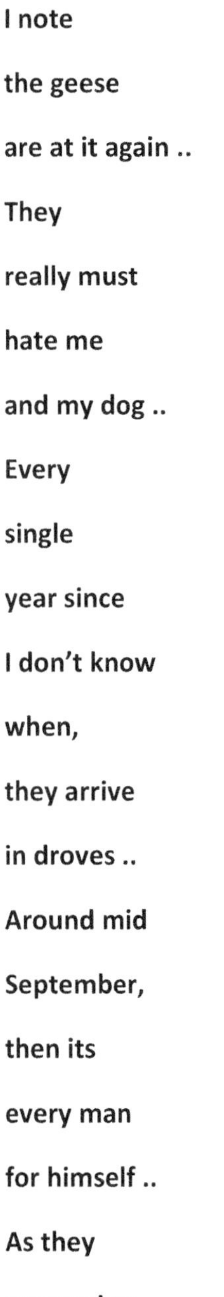

I note

the geese

are at it again ..

They

really must

hate me

and my dog ..

Every

single

year since

I don’t know

when,

they arrive

in droves ..

Around mid

September,

then its

every man

for himself ..

As they

proceed to

Echoes Don't Tell Lies

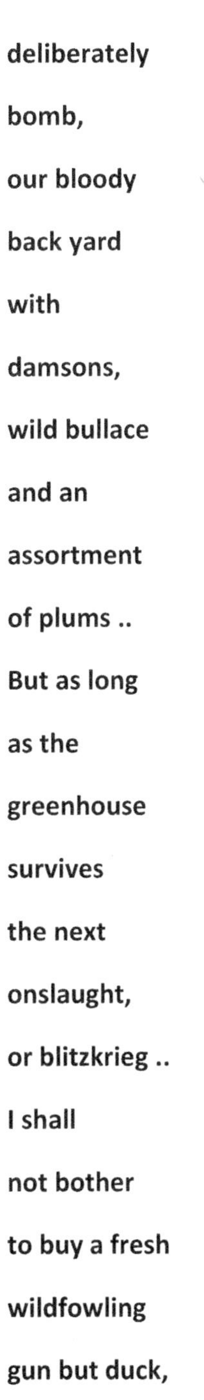

deliberately

bomb,

our bloody

back yard

with

damsons,

wild bullace

and an

assortment

of plums ..

But as long

as the

greenhouse

survives

the next

onslaught,

or blitzkrieg ..

I shall

not bother

to buy a fresh

wildfowling

gun but duck,

keep my

head down

and just

run for cover

when

the next

flight passes

over us ..

Peck drop

and run may

well sound

like a

kids game to

some ..

But around

these

here parts we

take it

dead serious ..

Me My Bro and A Chainsaw

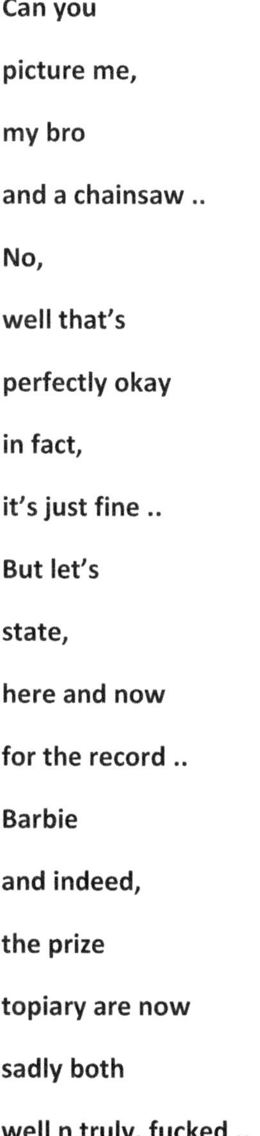

Can you

picture me,

my bro

and a chainsaw ..

No,

well that's

perfectly okay

in fact,

it's just fine ..

But let's

state,

here and now

for the record ..

Barbie

and indeed,

the prize

topiary are now

sadly both

well n truly, fucked ..

That Certain Something

It is almost

inconceivable

to imagine

these days ..

The might

and the sheer

intensity

of love which

almost

everyone felt

for him

back then ..

One can only

imagine,

it must have

felt much

like the first

flush of

love we each

had back

in the days

of our youth ..

But more

intense even,

if indeed

that was possible ..

When the Judge Says Swing

motive

unproven

but

guilty

as charged ..

he

shall swing

from

a bough

for a

year and a

day ..

The law is

an ass

m'lady what

more

can one say

the

judge got his

quota

at the end

of a long day ..

The Map

There was once

a time golden,

when it all came

together

and I would spell

your name

backwards quite

simply

because it made

it all seem

magic or special ..

And anyhow,

it was always so

very much

easier to find my

way home

when I wrote it

that way ..

Yes, there was

once a time golden,

when it all came

together ..

When we lived on

small talk,

free love and so

very much

laughter we often

ached all day ..

Back when we both

thought we

might last forever ..

But of course,

we never did, did we ..

When You Know You Are Blessed

When the queue

is down

to just one

and that one

just so happens

to be you ..

And

when the train

arrives

bang on time

and it

starts raining

the very

same second

you hop

on board ..

When the

outside toilet

seat

is still warm

to the touch ..

And

when you

look in your

new

grandchild's

eyes

and she smiles ..

Well

then you

just know that

you have

been blessed ..

Witcher's Eye

She hears

what she wants to hear

and is blind to everything else ..

Ghetto Girls

In order to survive,

they had to

acquire the imagination

of a ghetto whore

and quickly ..

Therefore, making out

the dark side

of arc lights and with

strangers,

for bread was easy ..

It was those late shift

oven duties

that made each of their

skins crawl

and stomachs turn ..

But it just had to be done ..

Womb Envy

They are all

very different, you know that

don't you, he said ..

What are,

wombs, he replied ..

Go on, get outa here ..

No honest,

it's as true

as the sky is blue ..

Claire's got

a heart shaped one

she told me herself ..

And Sues, is simply inverted

while our Jane's is kinda keyhole

shaped, but then she's perverted ..

Go on,

I'm intrigued now ..

Okay then, Jills is just perfect ..

Well what about

Angela and Emma's

just between you and me ..

Angela's is somewhat

spectacular and almost rectangular

while Emma, aint got one at all ..

Fancy that ..

No thanks, but I shall

no doubt look into it ..

So what about Jenny

she must keep her hand on her

ha'penny surely ..

Okay, so Jens is outstanding ..

What do you mean by that exactly ..

I mean it stands out a wee bit ..

Sod that for a game of soldiers,

I shall defo look into it,

how very interesting cheers bro ..

An Uncertain Kind of Aloneness

When we first met

her hair was

the same colour as

tropical sand

caressed by waves

and the sea ..

So when I close my

eyes slow now,

I can maybe still

find us,

on an empty beach

somewhere ..

And with any luck,

about to become

naked ..

Although we are

never alone are we ..

They just

placed a camera

and a microphone

inside the belly

of my mandolin ..

How else can they

possibly

continue to rape

and abuse us ..

Now that our pride

and dignity are gone ..

Dogmatism in Two Short Verses

we

all believe, simply

because we all want to believe ..

without believing, where would we all be ..

we would surely, be lost and surely, uncertain ..

but then, believe it or not, we would all gladly, be free ..

Shadow Dance

Even though clearly we

don't have

enough ink between

the two of us ..

Can you imagine for

one moment

the dance our tattoo's

might have made,

as we make love with

the sun, pinned

directly behind us to

the turquoise sky ..

And can you envisage

the dark of our

silhouette's as they do

cast freely their

individual shadows ..

And every single one

of them, is laughing out loud ..

Another Perfect Day

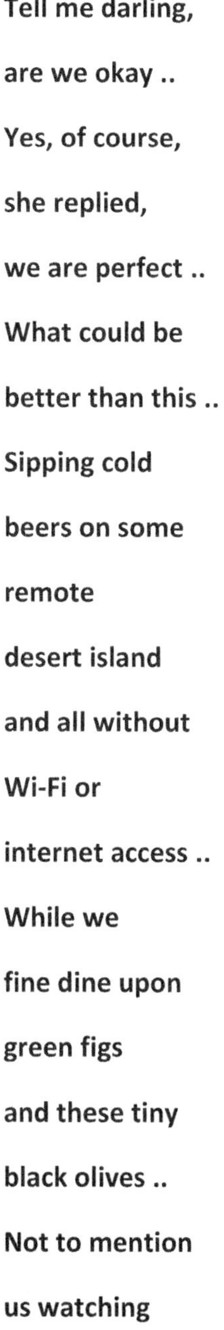

Tell me darling,

are we okay ..

Yes, of course,

she replied,

we are perfect ..

What could be

better than this ..

Sipping cold

beers on some

remote

desert island

and all without

Wi-Fi or

internet access ..

While we

fine dine upon

green figs

and these tiny

black olives ..

Not to mention

us watching

the fishermen

mending

their nets and

fighting off

all of the gulls ..

Then there's

me of course,

catching

an occasional

whiff from

a perfect grey

smoke ring ..

As it rises from

one of your

rare gauloises bleus ..

The Grieving Silence of An Empty House

When the silence

of their empty house

proved deafening ..

Instead of leaning in,

she turned away

from him and his kin ..

But it wasn't

always like that now

was it darling ..

And the key may yet

be found

just where he left it ..

Should she ever

need it again that is

or in case by some chance ..

A stranger might be

listening,

or wondering even ..

What they know

about loss, about lust,

about longing, or love even ..

Well Done

I don't want to be a cliché

or dance

with shadow children on

distant balconies ..

That's not what balconies

are for now, is it ..

I want to sit and watch you

read your kindle ..

While the sun goes down

and we both blister ..

Before that is, we each turn,

golden brown ..

All the Wrong Buttons

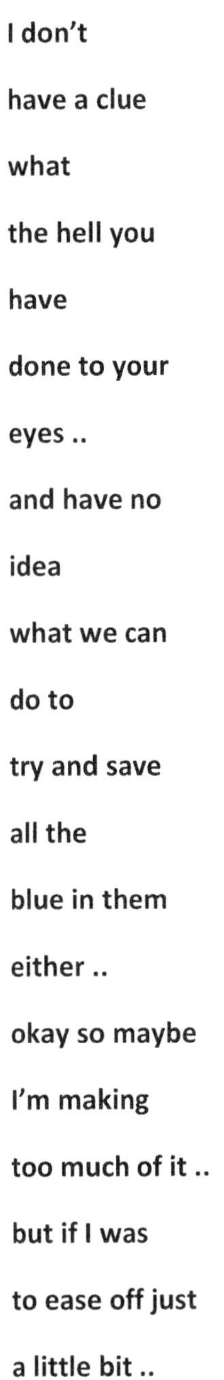

I don't

have a clue

what

the hell you

have

done to your

eyes ..

and have no

idea

what we can

do to

try and save

all the

blue in them

either ..

okay so maybe

I'm making

too much of it ..

but if I was

to ease off just

a little bit ..

Echoes Don't Tell Lies

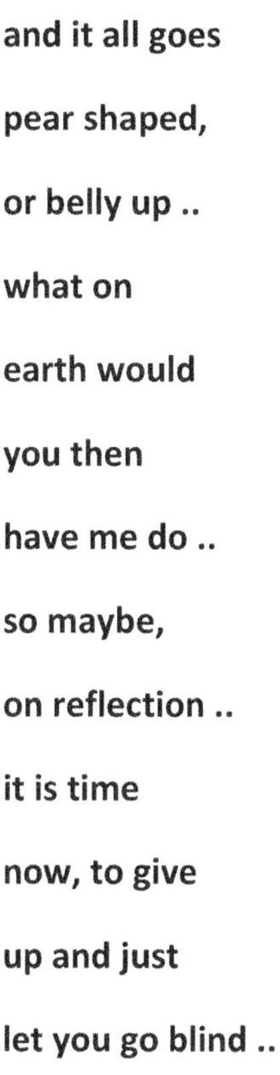

and it all goes

pear shaped,

or belly up ..

what on

earth would

you then

have me do ..

so maybe,

on reflection ..

it is time

now, to give

up and just

let you go blind ..

Neville Pettitt

Maybe it Must be Love

Since I can't seem to say her name

without smiling ..

I imagine, it must therefore be love ..

The Sound of Darkness

Listen,

can you hear

darkness forming ..

See how

the light it flickers ..

Take it

from me darling ..

That roar,

is not a sign from

up above ..

But surely, more

a mighty warning ..

Can you

feel it too, my love ..

I sense

a certain darkness

calling ..

Yet fear not, it feels

just like me

being called, back

home again ..

This is Not a Threat Okay

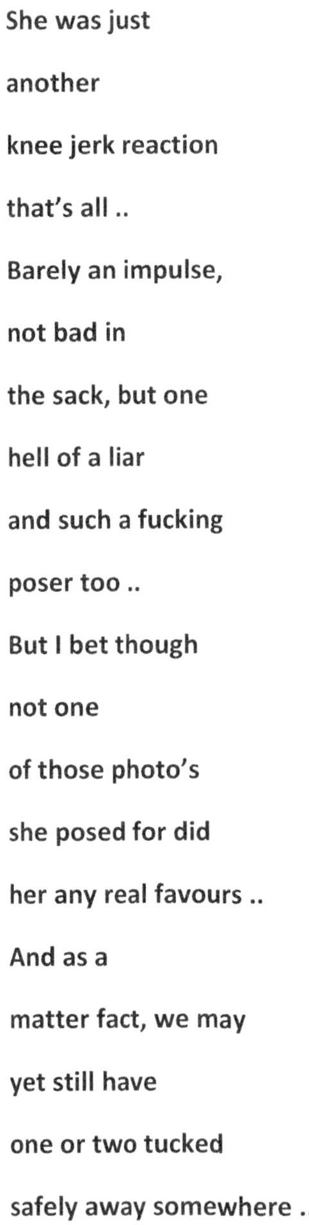

She was just

another

knee jerk reaction

that's all ..

Barely an impulse,

not bad in

the sack, but one

hell of a liar

and such a fucking

poser too ..

But I bet though

not one

of those photo's

she posed for did

her any real favours ..

And as a

matter fact, we may

yet still have

one or two tucked

safely away somewhere ..

Clean Breaks

Clean breaks are

always

the quickest

to heal ..

So just man up,

move on

and get over me

swiftly, she said ..

Breathe Easy

There will always

be those

who say otherwise ..

But we've got

your back covered ..

So now, you can

do almost anything ..

Skip through

your days and jump

as high as you

please, but always

land lightly my love ..

While the dark

days are now well

behind you,

there may yet be

occasional shadows ..

So relax, just pretend

they are rainbows

and breathe easy my love ..

Too Many Maybe's

While

his life seemed

so full

of maybe's ..

There

was barely

enough room

for a

single perhaps ..

Somewhere Down in The Hold

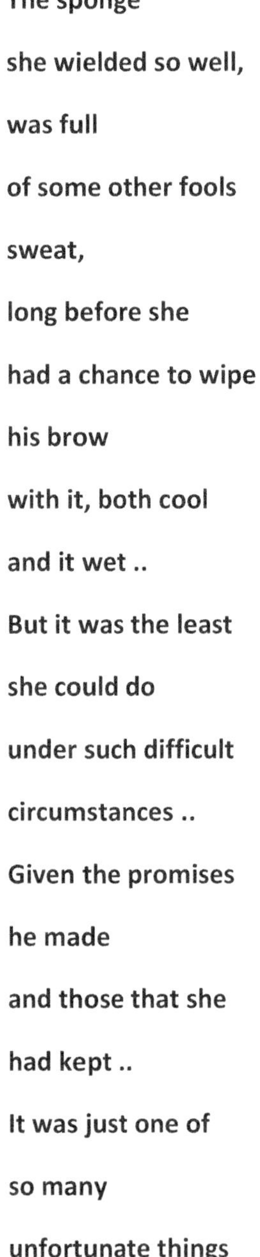

The sponge
she wielded so well,
was full
of some other fools
sweat,
long before she
had a chance to wipe
his brow
with it, both cool
and it wet ..
But it was the least
she could do
under such difficult
circumstances ..
Given the promises
he made
and those that she
had kept ..
It was just one of
so many
unfortunate things

Echoes Don't Tell Lies

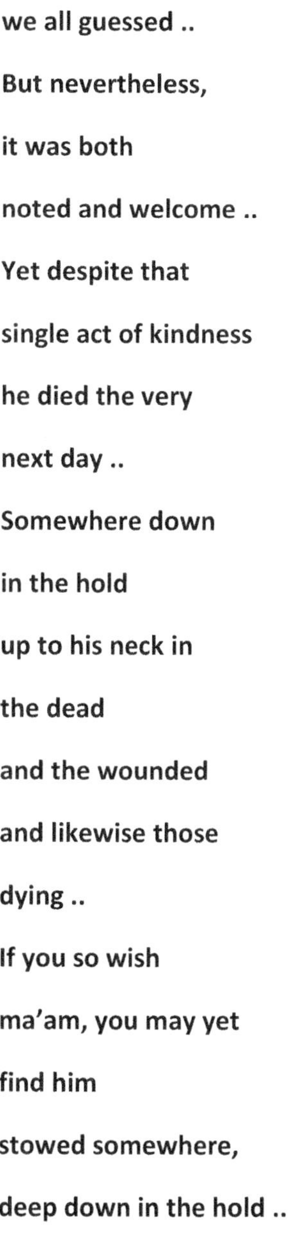

we all guessed ..

But nevertheless,

it was both

noted and welcome ..

Yet despite that

single act of kindness

he died the very

next day ..

Somewhere down

in the hold

up to his neck in

the dead

and the wounded

and likewise those

dying ..

If you so wish

ma'am, you may yet

find him

stowed somewhere,

deep down in the hold ..

When Sweet Talk Turns Sour

I don't wish to be

unkind

but boy, she's got

a dirty mind ..

And they of course,

all claim to

love her very much ..

Tho only for

one moment mind,

or maybe

two perhaps, in time

and not a

single second longer ..

In the Wake of a Wish

Maybe we can only

imagine ..

In the wake of a wish

and now wonder ..

But slowly,

just how good we

might once have been ..

Neville Pettitt

When All Said and Done it's All Over

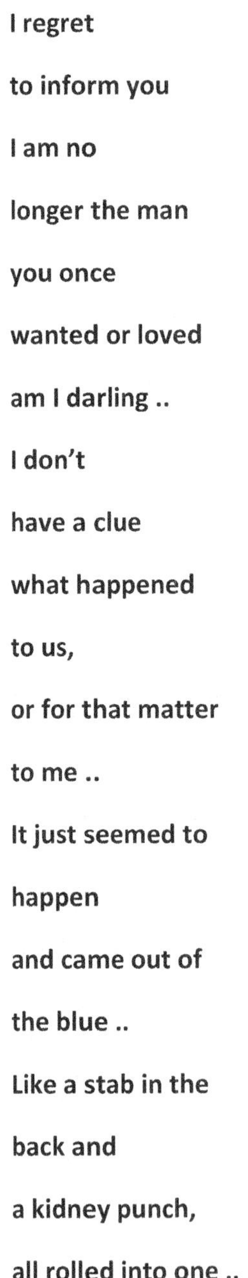

I regret

to inform you

I am no

longer the man

you once

wanted or loved

am I darling ..

I don't

have a clue

what happened

to us,

or for that matter

to me ..

It just seemed to

happen

and came out of

the blue ..

Like a stab in the

back and

a kidney punch,

all rolled into one ..

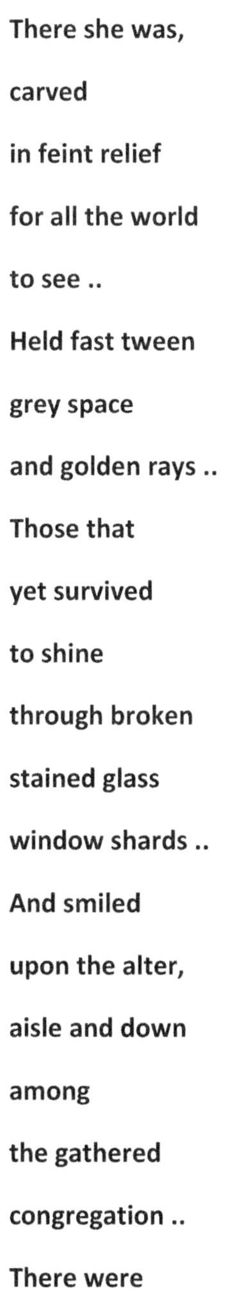

Mary

There she was,

carved

in feint relief

for all the world

to see ..

Held fast tween

grey space

and golden rays ..

Those that

yet survived

to shine

through broken

stained glass

window shards ..

And smiled

upon the alter,

aisle and down

among

the gathered

congregation ..

There were

of course those

among them,

who swore that

it was Mary ..

And one or two

even left

an extra penny

in the collection box ..

Muck Spreading

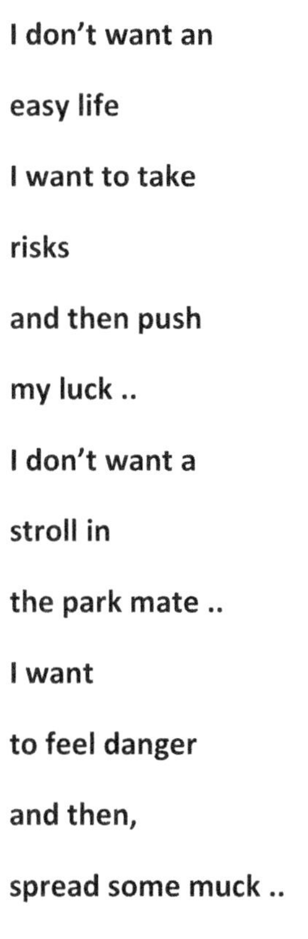

I don't want an

easy life

I want to take

risks

and then push

my luck ..

I don't want a

stroll in

the park mate ..

I want

to feel danger

and then,

spread some muck ..

Acid Days

When I lived in

a pyramid

you would feast

on dead bodies

and take

photographs

of dead crows

on a white sheet

against

a backdrop

of masturbating

angels ..

Today it seems

things

have moved on

quite a bit,

since the acid days ..

Ricardos Culinarium

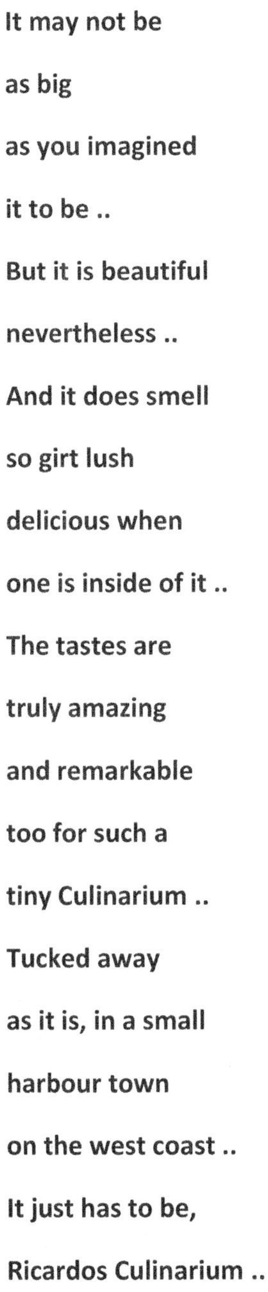

It may not be

as big

as you imagined

it to be ..

But it is beautiful

nevertheless ..

And it does smell

so girt lush

delicious when

one is inside of it ..

The tastes are

truly amazing

and remarkable

too for such a

tiny Culinarium ..

Tucked away

as it is, in a small

harbour town

on the west coast ..

It just has to be,

Ricardos Culinarium ..

One More Slice Should Do

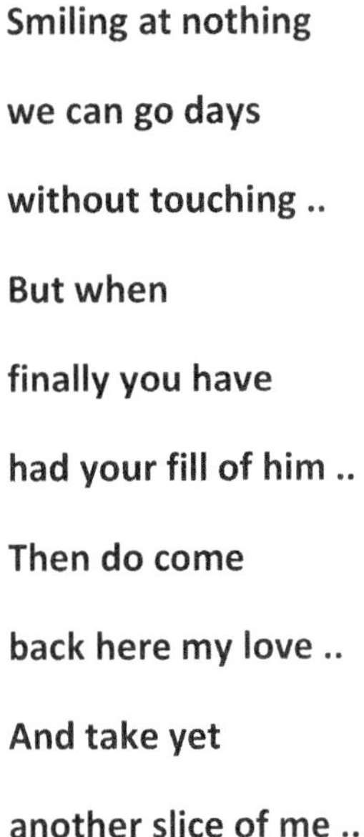

Smiling at nothing

we can go days

without touching ..

But when

finally you have

had your fill of him ..

Then do come

back here my love ..

And take yet

another slice of me ..

Marginally Slighted

Somewhere near

the steep hill,

there lies buried

deep within

a shallow grave

yet filled

to the very brim

they say

and overflowing,

with jealousy,

false hope,

lies and with rage

a woman scorned ..

Upon Those Words She Chose to Leave Behind

I did not

merely stumble blindly

upon

those words

she left behind in such

exquisite

and likewise,

well-rehearsed disarray ..

And nor

did I by any chance,

as you might well imagine,

upon her sudden,

unscheduled departure ..

Since we

both knew I would,

one day return,

to firstly kneel and then,

lay prone

beside them all ..

While quaffing each

last drop of them and so

very deeply ..

For it is there

I shall remain, till done ..

And thus,

my final abreaction is both

quietly and so

very solemnly completed ..

Indeed, then and only then,

dare I squeeze

that last drop of the poison in ..

The Dance of Overshadowed Children

The dance of overshadowed children,

above their shallow graves,

always takes place in the grey space

between dusk

and the break of a brand new day ..

Since that is always,

where and when, they all gather to cry ..

Orange Blossom Daze

orange blossom

always does it for me

whether upon

my arrival or eventual

departure ..

orange blossom always

does it for me

in so very many waze ..

Note there are no typo's on this page

Neville Pettitt

When Last Seen She Was Holding on Tightly

When last seen, she was clutching

a long thin

strip of navy blue velvet and near

bent double,

somewhere near to the grasp of

her middle ..

And in so doing she thus, allowed

the hem

of her slip, to go on public display ..

Oh' come

and sail with us, the sailors did sing ..

Yes come, see how

she swings like a brassed pendulum

sways ..

When last she was seen, she was seen

holding a

bottle green velvet, measure of satin ..

Fit for a lady,

or queen even, so fine a piece of cloth

it then was ..

Yet still, she was creased close to the

Echoes Don't Tell Lies

weave of her middle ..

And in so being, allowed the hem

of her fine

cotton camisole to splay, far too near

a torn seam,

somewhere down near the midline ..

And all of them

sailors did roar, come and play with us ..

This gall

she can pitch, like a galleon might pitch

in a raging

south westerly squall and when last she

was seen,

she was holding a new babe in both arms

all wrapped in a

dirty, cream coloured, silk shawl and both

appeared to be starving ..

And still the sailors did sing, come and play

with us lass,

we shall make it alright, come the morning ..

Accumulations

He, being a poet

and a collector of new words,

old stamps and gold coins ..

Just as she,

being adorable, collects new lovers,

bad losers and fools ..

While together,

they collected moments,

made love and changed history ..

On Moving On

should you ever find

another

lover which no doubt

you most

surely will when I am

gone ..

I could not for a single

moment

blame you for moving

on ..

though I would like to

think

you might think of me

every

now and then, maybe ..

On Top of Old Bones

They once made out

in a cemetery

on top of old bones ..

Not for a bet

you understand,

or because it just so

happened

to be Halloween ..

But for the hell of it ..

To her, he meant

nothing at all ..

He was just some

crazy kid ..

While she, was his

number seventeen ..

And just another

short lived ghoul friend ..

When My Heart Fell in Love

When my heart felt in love

all I could see

were roses and cardinals

and fresh laundered sheets ..

When my brain

was engaged, I could hear,

taste and smell

a desert, the ocean and sky ..

When my soul

was in synch with my spirit,

I just knew that I was free again ..

Neville Pettitt

So Very Much of a Muchness

Whether brown eyes
or blue,
both appear the same
to me these days ..
But I am not looking
for sympathy ..
It is just the way that
I see things, you see ..

Both your smile
and your frown look
much the same to me ..
But I don't want
even an ounce of your
sympathy ..
It is just where we
are standing these days ..

And while both
your love and disdain
feel the same to me ..
I don't want even a grain

of false sympathy ..

Since I know, beyond

knowing it would simply

be a precursor

to your eventual leading

and then, leaving me blindly ..

Ned's View

Just think

about it before

rejoicing,

that's all I ask ..

Before

I swing or not

and all

for the sake

of two stocking

frames

and a bloody

brand new loom ..

The world,

our world,

this world is no

better off

for most of it ..

And while they

call it

technology,

or progress ..

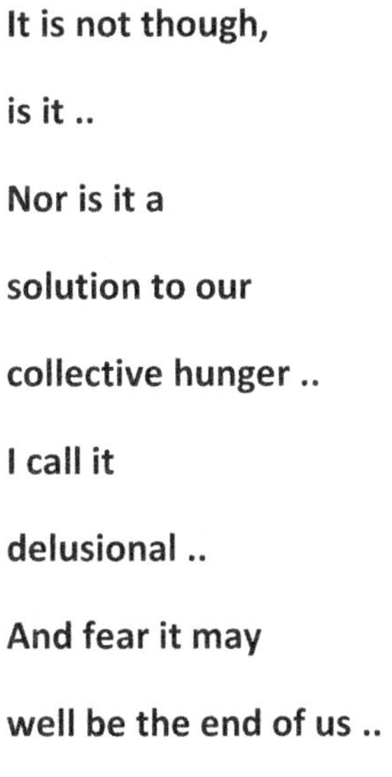

It is not though,

is it ..

Nor is it a

solution to our

collective hunger ..

I call it

delusional ..

And fear it may

well be the end of us ..

Neville Pettitt

It's Just a Question of Zen

when she lays down in a forest with

no one to hear her,

does she make more than a whisper or sigh

So Much More Than A Madness

Without antecedents

we have nothing,

but can still choose what

we want us to be ..

I know how to starve,

to deny

and to punish myself ..

But refuse

to eat rainbows or play

silly leaving games ..

I just need to know

how many resurrections

we are each

allowed these days ..

Without feeling

something missing inside ..

I really need to be

famous you see, for the

remaining fifteen

minutes, left of today ..

Feels Like There's a Stranger in the House

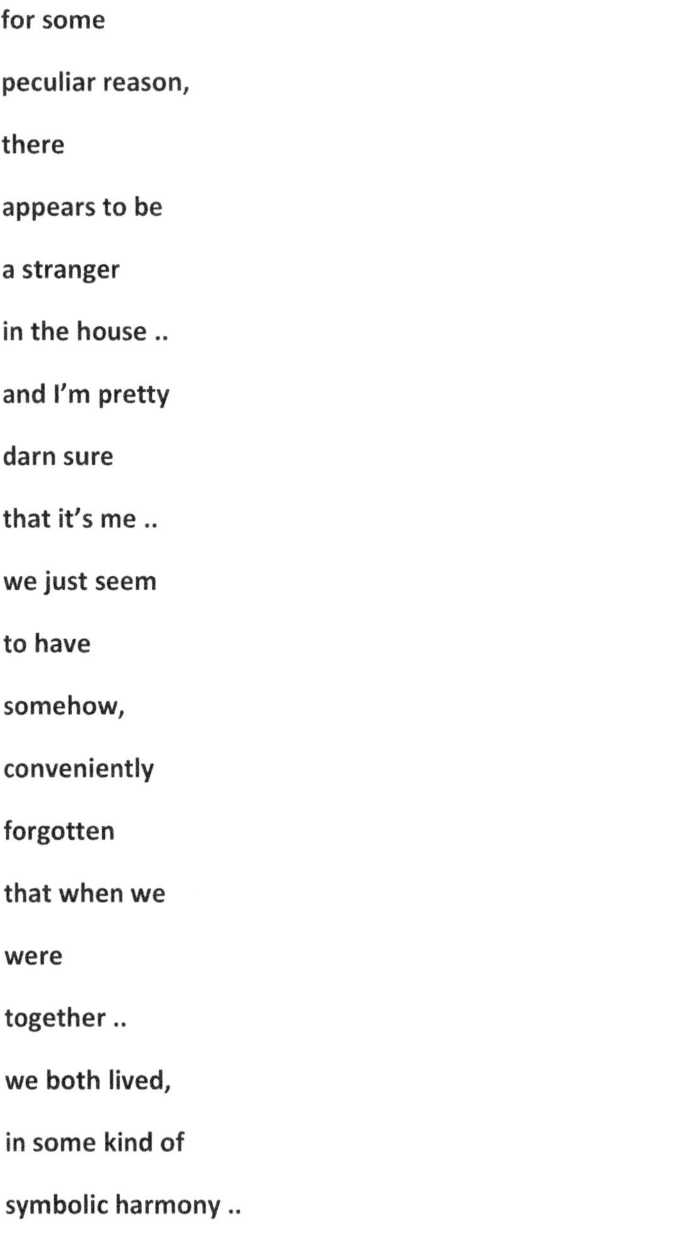

for some

peculiar reason,

there

appears to be

a stranger

in the house ..

and I'm pretty

darn sure

that it's me ..

we just seem

to have

somehow,

conveniently

forgotten

that when we

were

together ..

we both lived,

in some kind of

symbolic harmony ..

Our Newest of Sacraments

Once upon a time we

would have

stayed up all night

with just

a large a large glass

of red

and a small packet

of three

between two of us ..

My word,

how times change ..

Now it's

hop into bed right

after the news,

and a very small

mug of hot chocolate ..

Neville Pettitt

A Handful of Water

I watched,

but from a safe distance

and took note

of how you worked them

between your

rough, calloused and still

bleeding hands

until they were smoothe

like pebbles

or pretty polished glass ..

And my word,

how they glistened upon

the backs

and the palms of those

hands of yours ..

I recall how I marvelled

at how they

looked just like pearls,

but were mere

beads of water, yet no less

precious perhaps

than perfect cut diamonds

in this desolate

landscaped desert of ours ..

Silly Me

Silly me,

but long ago now ..

I once

threw each letter

of your name

and yes,

in the right order ..

Into an

old wishing well

and called

upon the gods to

grant me just one ..

Then I burnt

three small green

candles ..

Each with your

name carved upon ..

And swore

upon the graves

of those

I once loved

Echoes Don't Tell Lies

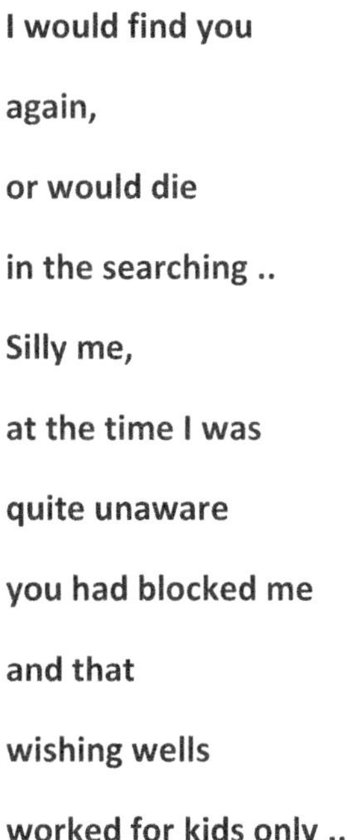

I would find you

again,

or would die

in the searching ..

Silly me,

at the time I was

quite unaware

you had blocked me

and that

wishing wells

worked for kids only ..

Talk About Stupid

Talk about stupid

when I first

caught your scent

in a shell ..

For one stupid

moment,

I thought I could

hear, feel

and taste you as well ..

Down In the Dunes

Back in the day,

she was so

much like

a new china doll,

and certainly

no less delicate ..

At first,

I thought I might

even break her ..

Just like

I once broke

the backs

and the spines

of all those

ever so fragile

and tiny,

sea creatures

which once

lived in the sand

where we

played and so

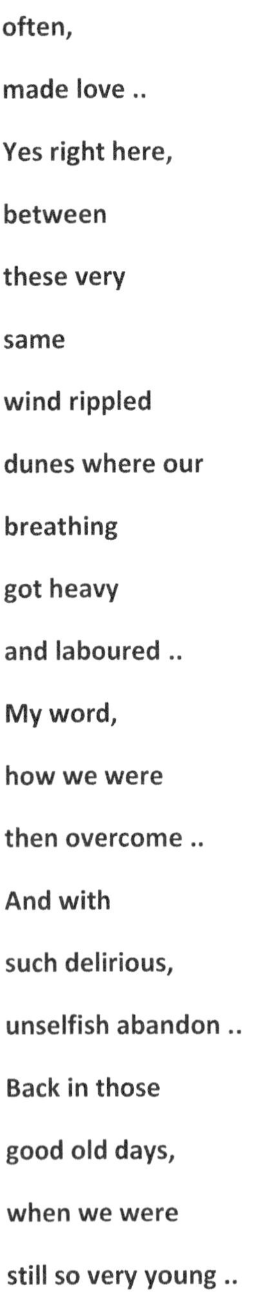

often,

made love ..

Yes right here,

between

these very

same

wind rippled

dunes where our

breathing

got heavy

and laboured ..

My word,

how we were

then overcome ..

And with

such delirious,

unselfish abandon ..

Back in those

good old days,

when we were

still so very young ..

In the Wake of One Hell of a Party

Hey, listen up, I want to be cremated,

but not just yet, okay ..

Although at the rate I am going

right now, if I don't have

some kind of heart attack before then ..

Around this same time

next year, or thereabouts, I shall be

pretty much dead anyway ..

So bring it all on, line up the beers and

the cream cakes, let's have

a premorbid party, before it's too late ..

Conchetta - Voice of the Sea

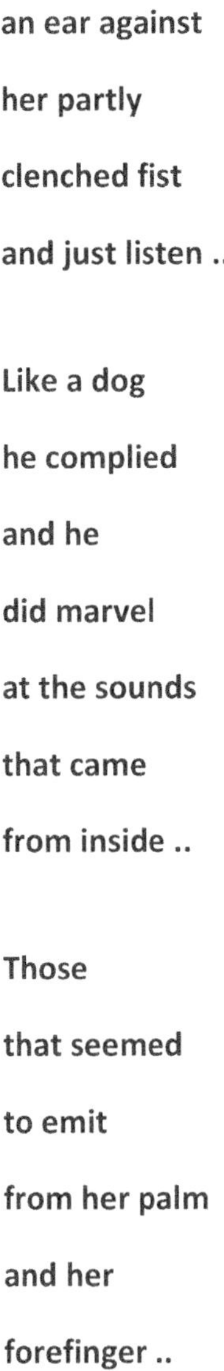

She bade him

come near,

then to place

an ear against

her partly

clenched fist

and just listen ..

Like a dog

he complied

and he

did marvel

at the sounds

that came

from inside ..

Those

that seemed

to emit

from her palm

and her

forefinger ..

Echoes Don't Tell Lies

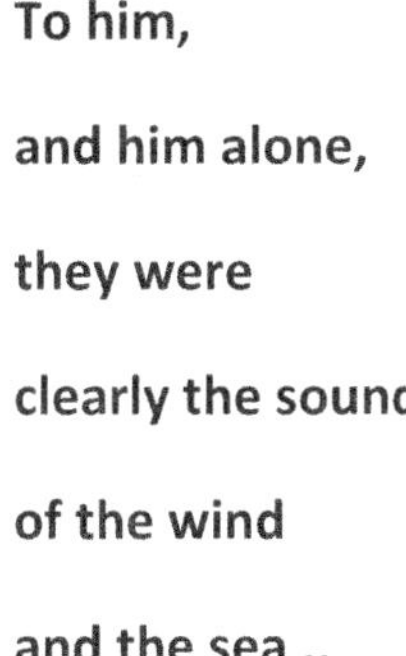

To him,

and him alone,

they were

clearly the sound

of the wind

and the sea ..

And it seems

it was then,

that he knelt at

her feet

and he begged

her to

make him

her slave again ..

Neville Pettitt

Don't Suppose You Remember

I don't suppose,

for a single

moment after

all these years ..

You still recall

a series

of otherwise

insignificant

coincidences ..

All of which,

I hasten to add

occurred

within a micro

second, or less

of me

calling out your

name ..

If it helps at all,

it was

the very same

Echoes Don't Tell Lies

day I talked

to a wall

about our love ..

And I swear

that it heard me

but blindly ..

That was when

a dream catcher

caught you

and the wind

chimes

chimed for me ..

Neville Pettitt

The Sense of Something, Before it is, Something

At the end of the day

it is not only

the daring to look,

but the finding

that really matters,

isn't it my darling ..

For instance,

take the silver

off white glint

on a herons cheek ..

Visible only

in the half-light,

or the tremor of

a single leaf rejoicing,

the moment

it shakes off that last

drop of rain,

before fall and is free

once more ..

And what about

Echoes Don't Tell Lies

the apple smell

of a tap room, lingering ..

And that of

new puppies, young

babies and old

scent bottles found

in attics

and long lost

camphor trunks

by chance ..

Or that, of the smell

trapped between

pages of old books

kept in libraries,

out of reach of both

prying eyes

and too tiny fingers ..

While the sound

of cracked church bells,

nightingales,

and worms turning

cut through the air

and compete with that

of snow drops

emerging ..

And can then, be heard

in the distance

above the cry of gulls

and storm clouds

forming ..

Come tell me darling

what on earth,

are we each missing ..

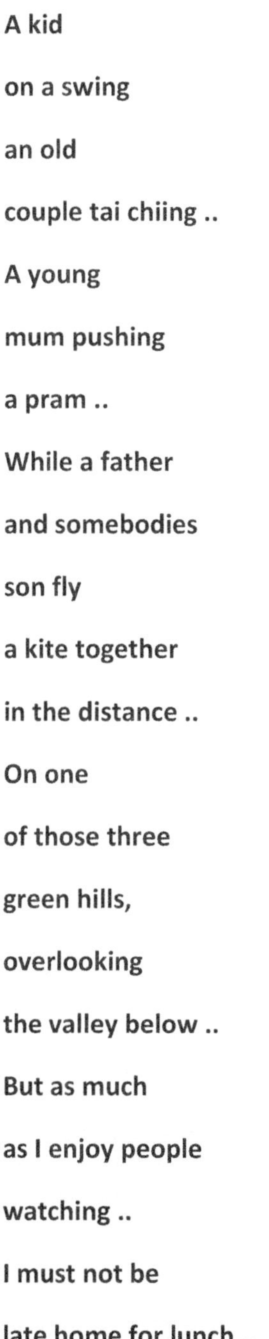

View Before Lunch

A kid

on a swing

an old

couple tai chiing ..

A young

mum pushing

a pram ..

While a father

and somebodies

son fly

a kite together

in the distance ..

On one

of those three

green hills,

overlooking

the valley below ..

But as much

as I enjoy people

watching ..

I must not be

late home for lunch ..

Neville Pettitt

Advice on Learning to Fall

Remember

my lovely,

to always run fast

and run free ..

And don't ever

be afraid

tho' my darling,

to jump high ..

But remember

my lovely,

to always land

lightly and roll with it ..

Sighing Over Spilt Milk

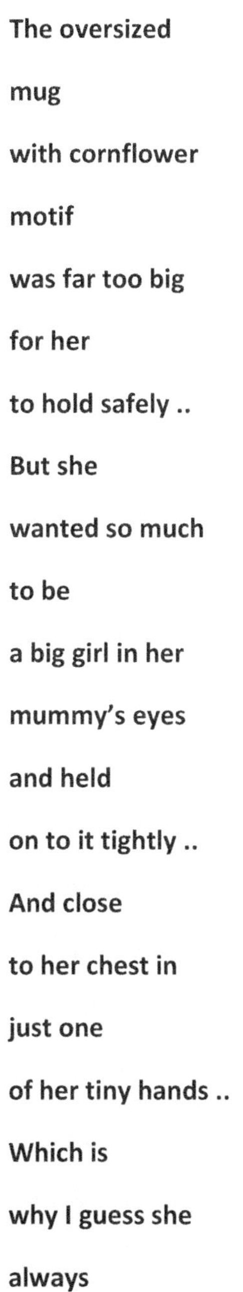

The oversized

mug

with cornflower

motif

was far too big

for her

to hold safely ..

But she

wanted so much

to be

a big girl in her

mummy's eyes

and held

on to it tightly ..

And close

to her chest in

just one

of her tiny hands ..

Which is

why I guess she

always

tends to get milk

in her

porridge and her

porridge

in both ears

and all over her hair ..

Leftovers

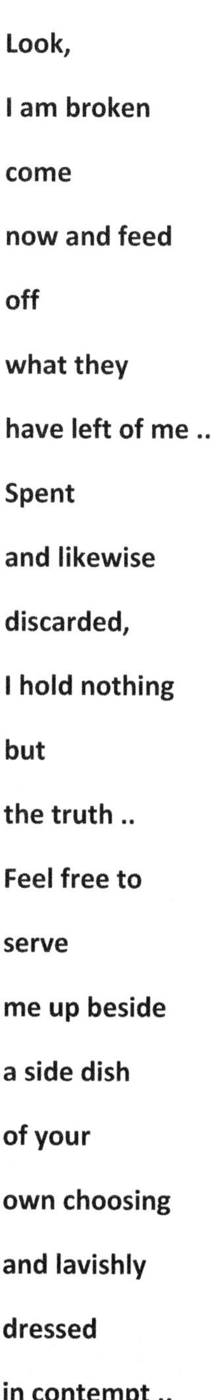

Look,

I am broken

come

now and feed

off

what they

have left of me ..

Spent

and likewise

discarded,

I hold nothing

but

the truth ..

Feel free to

serve

me up beside

a side dish

of your

own choosing

and lavishly

dressed

in contempt ..

Neville Pettitt

Another Near Empty Page

then there are days

when all that has passed

seems to fade into

another near empty page ..

Miss Match

It was perfectly clear

from the off,

they had one too

many dramas

between them both ..

It was time

to take a raincheck

and while he was

as hard as

a blacksmiths arm ..

She was

without doubt

more than his match

and twice as strong ..

And she

never lost a single

argument

the whole time they

were together ..

But if the truth was

known ..

They never really

had that long

together anyway

since it was

over long before

it had barely begun ..

Some loves

are not meant to be ..

Mirrors Don't Care Do They Darling

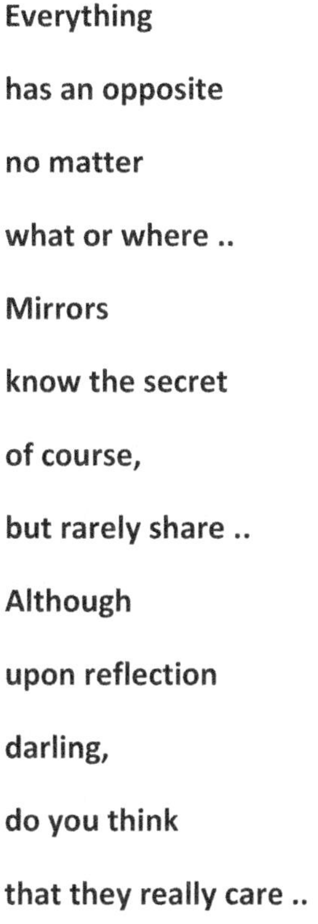

Everything

has an opposite

no matter

what or where ..

Mirrors

know the secret

of course,

but rarely share ..

Although

upon reflection

darling,

do you think

that they really care ..

That Afterwards Feeling

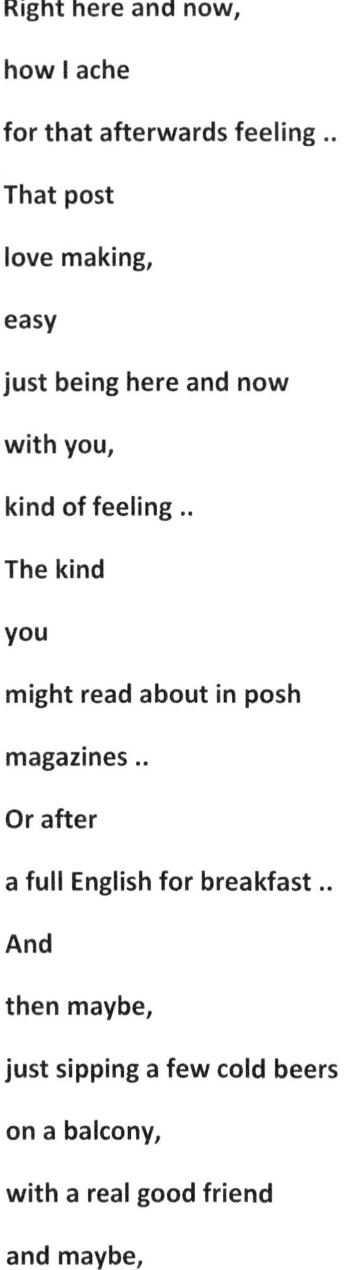

Right here and now,

how I ache

for that afterwards feeling ..

That post

love making,

easy

just being here and now

with you,

kind of feeling ..

The kind

you

might read about in posh

magazines ..

Or after

a full English for breakfast ..

And

then maybe,

just sipping a few cold beers

on a balcony,

with a real good friend

and maybe,

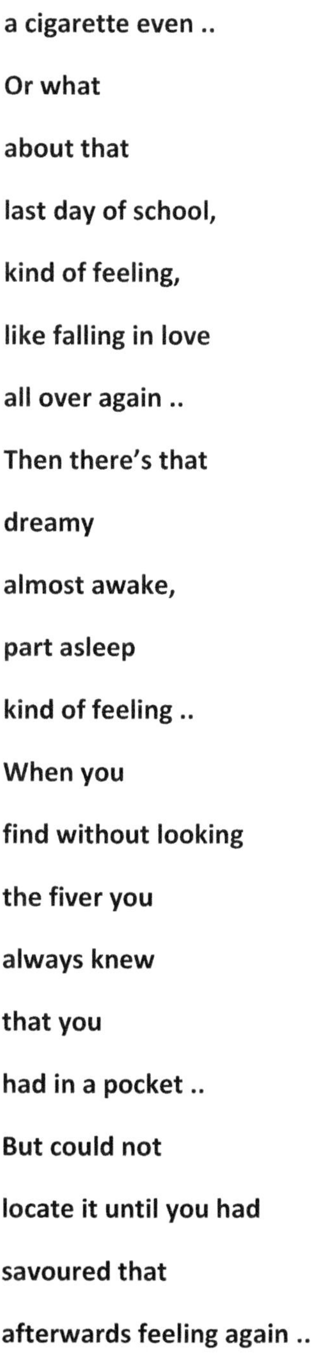

a cigarette even ..

Or what

about that

last day of school,

kind of feeling,

like falling in love

all over again ..

Then there’s that

dreamy

almost awake,

part asleep

kind of feeling ..

When you

find without looking

the fiver you

always knew

that you

had in a pocket ..

But could not

locate it until you had

savoured that

afterwards feeling again ..

Who Did What

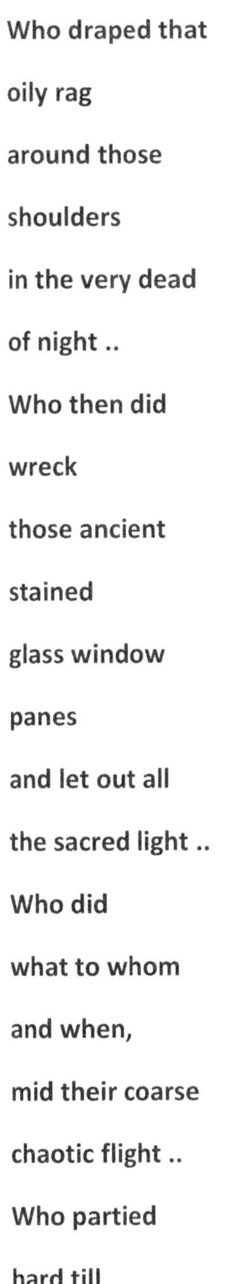

Who draped that

oily rag

around those

shoulders

in the very dead

of night ..

Who then did

wreck

those ancient

stained

glass window

panes

and let out all

the sacred light ..

Who did

what to whom

and when,

mid their coarse

chaotic flight ..

Who partied

hard till

Echoes Don't Tell Lies

mid December

and gave

up the ghost

without a fight ..

Then left

us wondering,

who did what ..

This is Us ..

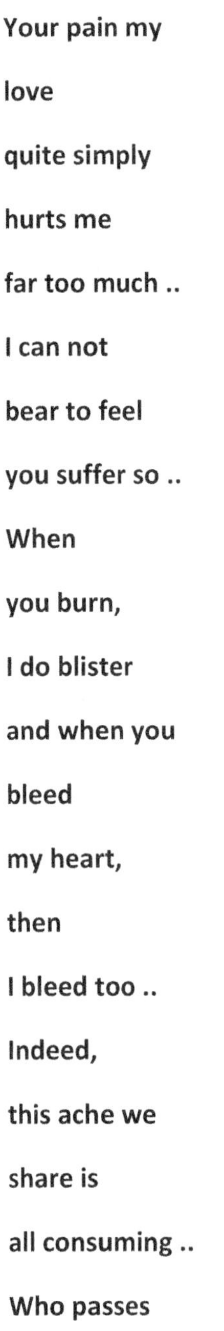

Your pain my

love

quite simply

hurts me

far too much ..

I can not

bear to feel

you suffer so ..

When

you burn,

I do blister

and when you

bleed

my heart,

then

I bleed too ..

Indeed,

this ache we

share is

all consuming ..

Who passes

Echoes Don’t Tell Lies

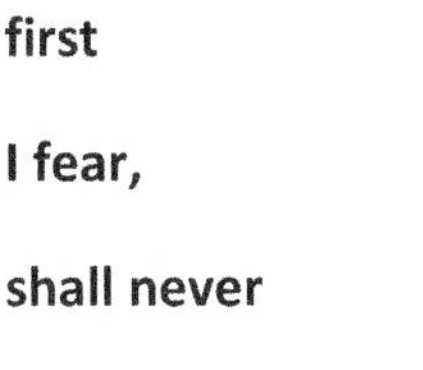

first

I fear,

shall never

let the other go ..

Now Looking Back With Anticipation

Slow down child

don't wish

your life away

like that ..

We know its late

but the cogs

and the wheels

are still turning ..

And while

I dare not look

back to see

what the future

might hold

by consulting

the leaves in my

new china

teacup darling ..

Each swirling

earl grey

murmeration

that I previously

found there ..

Now fills me

to the very brim

with much

love and indeed,

joyful anticipation ..

Going Against the Flow

Why stare at me

like that

my darling with

such ice cold

apprehension ..

A singular

detachment

if ever there was ..

Don't dare

tell me that you

think you

were misread,

by any chance ..

How on earth

did we arrive here

like this ..

And while at it,

pray tell ..

Why have you

now deserted me

and no longer

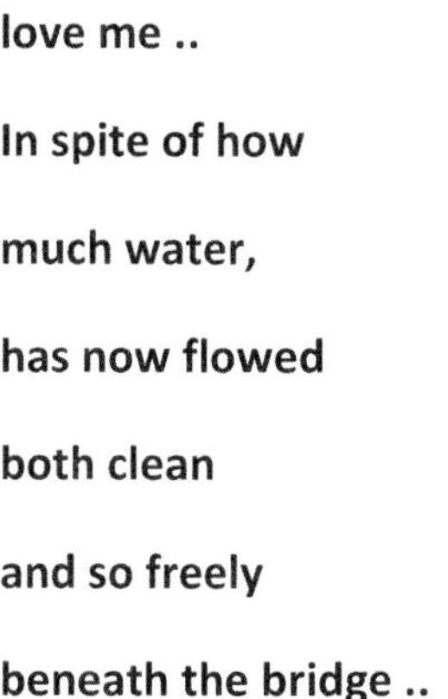

love me ..

In spite of how

much water,

has now flowed

both clean

and so freely

beneath the bridge ..

Neville Pettitt

Twisted History an Account of the Rape and Destruction of the Plains People

Having finally managed

to remove

the sharpest of jagged

shards from

distant high mountains

and carrying

them home with him ..

He made fire in a hollow

with dry weeds

and the leaves he took

from some

faraway forest which lies

somewhere

beyond the great grey

tumbling river ..

Then he burnt both sage

and saffron

to heal and to colour his

rage and his anger ..

In the wake of the rape

of his people

and all those whom he

loved

and the land he revered ..

Then later

in silence he fashioned

so many

straight arrows from flint

he had

stored and hid in his tepee ..

The rest

is now history, albeit twisted ..

Yet before

they eventually crucified him,

they said

it was a massacre and called

him a savage ..

Prophets of War

There are no clean
or pretty wars
are there darling ..
By definition,
each is ugly, filthy
and downright dirty ..
There are no
lessons to be learnt
at all from them ..
We have proved that
to ourselves,
time and time again
my friend ..
There is no point
in choosing sides,
or deny, who is
to fucking blame ..
There are no victors
or victories to
be won in this game ..
Shame on them,

but there is no point

in pointing

random pointy fingers

in any vague

direction, since each

of us shall be

losers in the long run ..

And the only

profiteers from war are

politicians, rats,

flies and other despots ..

Rest Assured

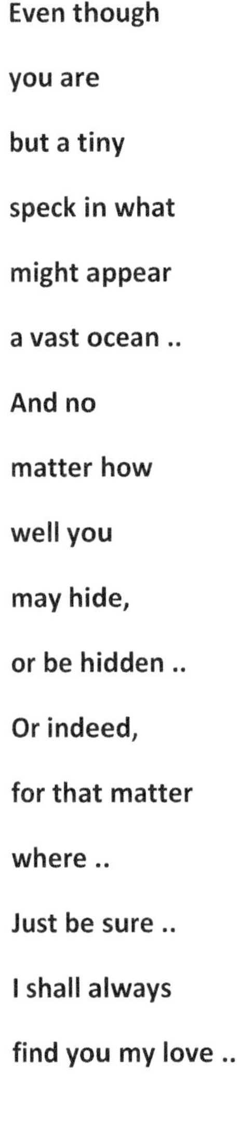

Even though

you are

but a tiny

speck in what

might appear

a vast ocean ..

And no

matter how

well you

may hide,

or be hidden ..

Or indeed,

for that matter

where ..

Just be sure ..

I shall always

find you my love ..

Just In Case You Are Ever Wrong

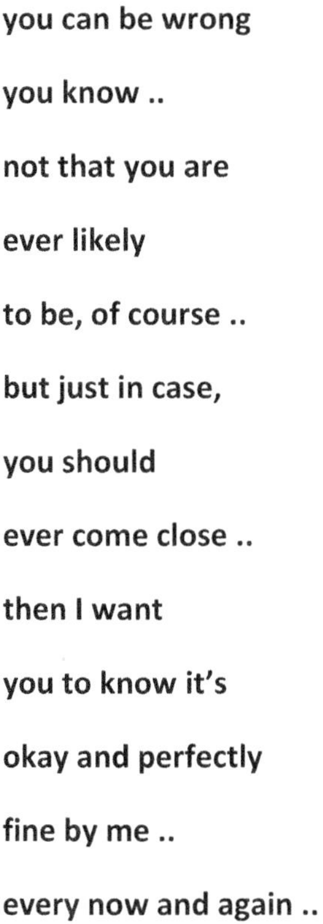

you can be wrong

you know ..

not that you are

ever likely

to be, of course ..

but just in case,

you should

ever come close ..

then I want

you to know it's

okay and perfectly

fine by me ..

every now and again ..

Not All Questions Have Answers

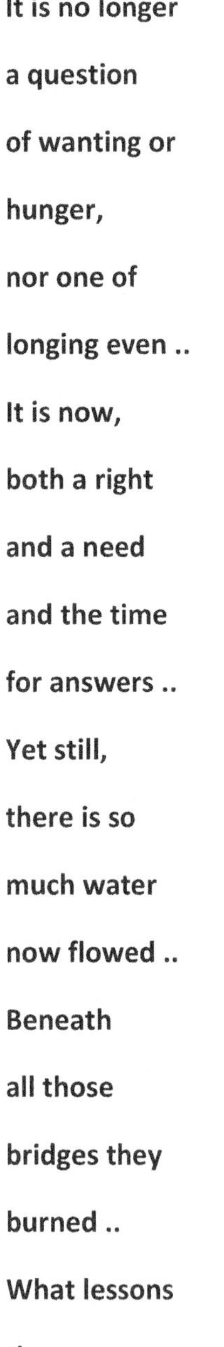

It is no longer

a question

of wanting or

hunger,

nor one of

longing even ..

It is now,

both a right

and a need

and the time

for answers ..

Yet still,

there is so

much water

now flowed ..

Beneath

all those

bridges they

burned ..

What lessons

they may

have once

learned, as yet

remain

to outsiders ..

Something of

a great mystery ..

Neville Pettitt

Do You Remember When

Do you remember

back when the world was so easy

and we were so young ..

Back when everything was so crazy

but oh’ so very much fun ..

I know I do and by the look in your eyes

I’m pretty sure, you do too ..

Haiku 4 Having Me She Said

while widows may peek

and wives they do worry so

young virgins wonder ..

Neville Pettitt

Genuine Fakes Sold Dirt Cheap

Look at how those

trees

slope at an angle

all the way down

to the side

of that lake over

there ..

Jeez you guys ..

don't you think

they look just like

T.S Lowries ..

And look at those

skyscrapers,

each stroke

of his brush leaves

behind ..

That guys a genius ..

Who else

could make whole

run of the mill,

street scenes come

alive like that ..

Each stick man, dog,

cat woman or child

is a little

masterpiece in its

own right ..

Yesterday he was

knocking out

huge self-portraits

by Van Goch

and some other guy

from Paris ..

Tomorrow it maybe

Turner's

turn, who knows,

or a little

Rembrandt perhaps ..

He must

surely make a small

fortune

each day, selling

genuine

fakes like that, to all

these filthy rich

tourists hereabouts ..

At the Very End of All My Tunnels

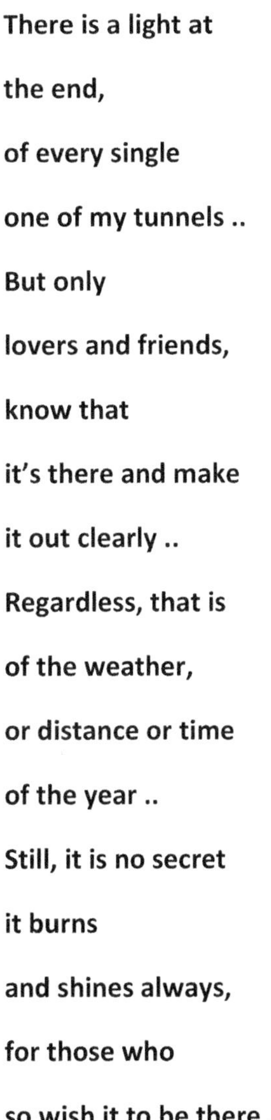

There is a light at

the end,

of every single

one of my tunnels ..

But only

lovers and friends,

know that

it's there and make

it out clearly ..

Regardless, that is

of the weather,

or distance or time

of the year ..

Still, it is no secret

it burns

and shines always,

for those who

so wish it to be there ..

Hold It, Swill Then Swallow

When my mind starts to wander

of its own accord,

which it seems to do increasingly ..

I might just wonder,

if you ever think back to the day

when I begged half a cup

of single malt, from a neighbour ..

Indeed, I still query

what he may have thought of me

back then, had I told him

it was not for me, but for the cavity

that kept you up

all night long and in so much agony ..

Somewhere Beyond Our Goodbyes

Look beyond the symmetry

of a perfect horizon

and note how the silver edge

arcs along those

shifting, unfamiliar lines,

like a smile arches upwards ..

Come walk with me

and let us sip the moments ..

Let us each rejoice

and ache together for soon,

the tide, shall turn against us ..

And then, we shall go

our separate ways, with just

a sorry farewell wave,

yet such, exquisite memories ..

And All Before Our First Awakening

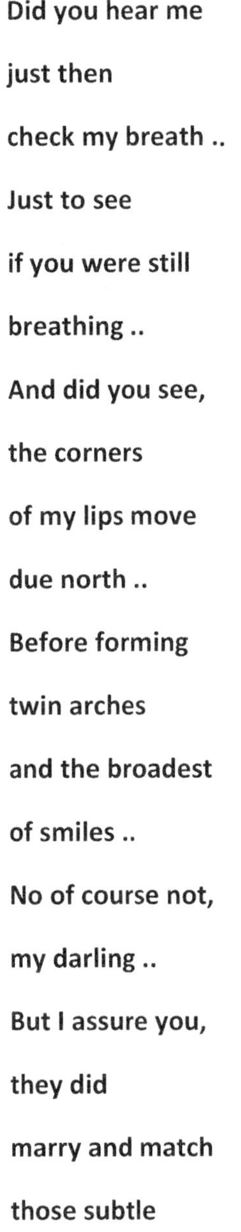

Did you hear me

just then

check my breath ..

Just to see

if you were still

breathing ..

And did you see,

the corners

of my lips move

due north ..

Before forming

twin arches

and the broadest

of smiles ..

No of course not,

my darling ..

But I assure you,

they did

marry and match

those subtle

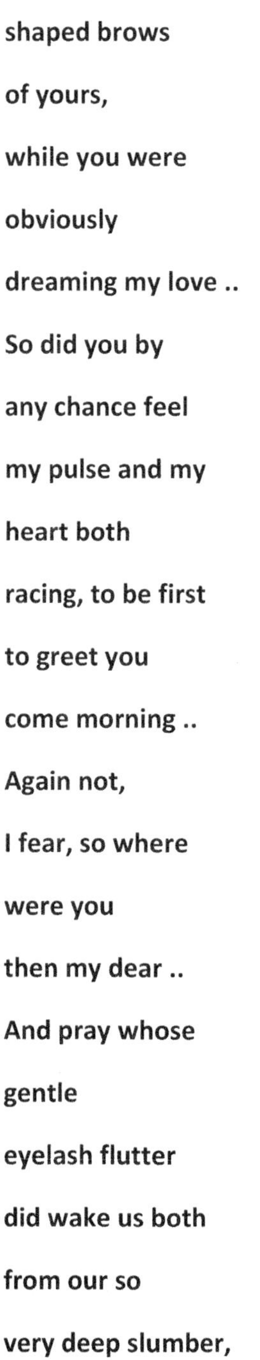

shaped brows
of yours,
while you were
obviously
dreaming my love ..
So did you by
any chance feel
my pulse and my
heart both
racing, to be first
to greet you
come morning ..
Again not,
I fear, so where
were you
then my dear ..
And pray whose
gentle
eyelash flutter
did wake us both
from our so
very deep slumber,

on the occasion

of this,

our first truly

shared morning ..

Amen

Would you believe

I forgot

if I said my prayers

before bed

and again, upon my

awakening ..

I fear I might just be

subliminally

damned and no, not

sublimely ..

That would be a fine

thing now

wouldn't it babe,

he says, smiling bigly

Amen ..

Behold All My Literary Demons

Hey you, listen to me ..

I am already

just a little bit dead

and the rest

of me is just dying ..

So for those

who might choose

to visit, be warned ..

I am not just

typing out words

metaphorically ..

Since I am sure what

will eventually

remain behind of me,

shall be none other

than my literary demons ..

You Can Always Tell When the End is Nigh

I do love you,

she said ..

I love you too,

he replied ..

Well

okay then but,

I'm sure,

I love you

much more ..

Well

maybe just

lately,

you do he

sighed slow ..

And they

both roll over

and sleep

until morning ..

He facing

the window

and her,

facing the door ..

Neville Pettitt

What a Question to Ask

When you get to the end of the line,

what do you intend to leave behind ..

Other than a full stop, or two, that is ..

What He Really Wants

I really don't want any

of that crazy

artificial intelligence stuff ..

I want new stem cell eyes

and another pair of knees ..

Oh' plus an end to hunger,

war and disease

and maybe a lottery win ..

Tu Es Tout Pour Moi

Oh' how I ache,

for all those

things you do gift

but are yet still,

to be remembered ..

And how I do

long for the scent

and the sense

of you near

and all around me ..

Yes and how

I do bleed into

sand, dust and dirt

and again,

upon rainbows ..

And all for the sake

of saving a pair

of honour and souls ..

But how you

do frown when I lay

down beside you

and exclaim that yes,

I do indeed love thee ..

Neville Pettitt

Dare to Stray

along the way

one shall inevitably encounter

occasional and inevitable diversions ..

sometimes, it makes more sense and is safer to

ignore them and to deviate on one's own terms and time ..

Famous Chat Up Lies

I don't wish to stare

but don't want to blink either ..

Through some irrational fear

of losing a single moment of you ..

And while I don't wish

to teach my granny to suck eggs ..

These words, as an icebreaker,

at singles events, bus stops or parties etc ..

Tend to work far better

than anything else, I have tried to date ..

Neville Pettitt

No Comment

Sitting there like that
with knees to chin
and blond hair strewn
still damp,
about her shoulders ..
Just like some
feathered well-worn
shawl and fresh from
her shower,
but still shaking ..
She was such a very
pretty sight regardless
of the bruises ..
Yes those, she tried so
hard to hide
neath well-rehearsed
yet shallow smile
and borrowed bath robe ..
The last time she
wore a matching pair
of cigarette burns,

like those, worn today ..

When asked

how she acquired them ..

Yet once again

replied, no comment ..

How Many Ways Precisely

How many ways

might one be

loved and truly ..

From a distance,

maybe or

up close, full on

and presumably,

in so many

other ways tooly ..

Oh' yes indeed

how many ways

not vaguely

or even remotely

but precisely my love ..

Upon Leaving One's Shadow Behind

Together we shall

defy both mirrors

and darkness

and live together

forever in gardens ..

But don't you dare

suffer in silence

my precious,

instead let me in ..

We need to break

bread and to share

all of these gifts

we have been given ..

Unless you are on

some kind of

mission and driven

to discredit,

and then shaming

yours truly ..

Which surely would,

I imagine, feel more

like chasing

and killing your own

precious shadow ..

By the simple act,

of starving it of all light ..

A Snog is For Life Not Just for Christmas

My word,

how we kissed back

then ..

Until both our

tongues

ached and then they

became

delightfully numbed ..

I also recall

your breath and how

it always

tasted so minty fresh ..

With an

aftertaste I just can't

put my finger on ..

I used to

smoke Marlboro's

back then ..

So can't imagine or

rather,

don't want to Imagine

Neville Pettitt

what mine

must have tasted of ..

But it must

have been love surely ..

Rebecca's Got Her Grandma's Chuckle

I do so love that grandma chuckle

you inherited Bex ..

I could listen and laugh with you

all day, every day ..

But you got a little bird to look after

so save me for another rainy day ..

Neville Pettitt

A Unity of Opposites

They say that opposites attract don't they ..

But a moth, is not the opposite of a flame is it ..

So where does all the fascination come from ..

Floating Down On a Whisper

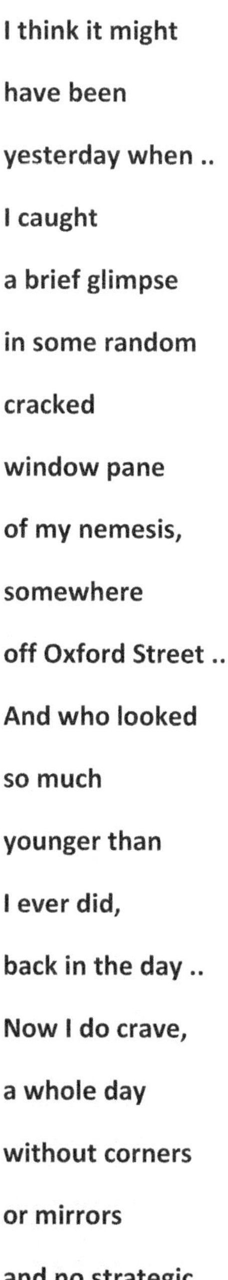

I think it might

have been

yesterday when ..

I caught

a brief glimpse

in some random

cracked

window pane

of my nemesis,

somewhere

off Oxford Street ..

And who looked

so much

younger than

I ever did,

back in the day ..

Now I do crave,

a whole day

without corners

or mirrors

and no strategic

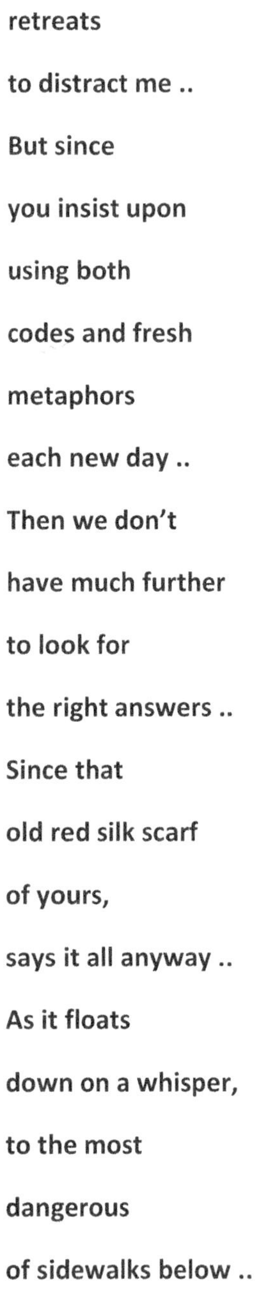

retreats

to distract me ..

But since

you insist upon

using both

codes and fresh

metaphors

each new day ..

Then we don't

have much further

to look for

the right answers ..

Since that

old red silk scarf

of yours,

says it all anyway ..

As it floats

down on a whisper,

to the most

dangerous

of sidewalks below ..

Things Well Remembered

The way she ate her ice cream,

the way she picked at cheese ..

The way she wore his Tee shirt,

all those ways, she tried to please ..

Neville Pettitt

Almost Famous Last Words

Although this heart be stilled

the world still spins

albeit slow and now much darker ..

Something About the Author

Having worked for many years as a Clinical Specialist, within the diverse field of adult mental health and substance misuse services across Northamptonshire, in Leicestershire and in Somerset. I have learnt that it is not necessarily the route or the direction we undertake throughout the course of our lives that is most important, or even the destination for that matter. But rather, it is those situations, circumstances and events we each encounter and often, take for granted along the way that which help to shape each and every one of us into a uniquely complex and individual human being.

Indeed, as such, I hope that some of my own personal observations and experiences have been captured and are likewise reflected here, in this, my tenth collection of poetry to date and which of course, I sincerely hope you enjoy.

Many thanks though, for daring to take a peek and regardless ..

All Good Things,

Neville

Acknowledgements

Front & rear cover photograph courtesy of the amazing Maternity Department at Musgrove Park Hospital, Taunton England and of course, the good old NHS. Used here, with the kind permission of both my daughter Rebecca and her husband Aaron ..

The rear cover inset photo, is of me, in a Somerset pub garden by the coast not too far from where I live. It was taken, shortly after the third national Covid 19 lockdown, by a dear friend, Lizzy Luvbug ..

Finally, my very special thanks go to each of the individuals and likewise, all those situations, circumstances and or events I alluded to earlier, that have either directly, or indirectly served to provide some inspiration for so many of these scribbles contained herein ..